St Elizabeth's

Dealing with sick kids can be heartbreaking,
funny, and uplifting, often all at once!

This series takes a look at a hospital set up
especially to deal with such children,
peeping behind the scenes into almost all the
departments and clinics, exploring the
problems and solutions of various diseases,
while watching the staff fall helplessly
in love—with the kids and with each other.

Enjoy!

Although a Lancastrian by birth, **Sheila Danton** has now settled in the West Country with her husband. Her nursing career, which took her to many parts of England, left her with 'itchy feet' which she indulges by travelling both at home and abroad. She uses her trips to discover new settings for her books, and also to visit their three grown-up children, who have flown the nest in different directions.

Recent titles by the same author:

Shared Responsibility
Dangerous Practice
Base Principles
Monsoons Apart
Prescription for Change
A Private Affair
Doctor's Dilemma
A Growing Trust
The Family Touch
Good Husband Material

ENDURING ATTRACTION

Sheila Danton

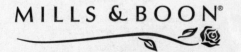

MILLS & BOON®

The author is very grateful to Yvonne Nichols in the
Outpatient Department of Bristol Royal Hospital for
Sick Children, and the staff, patients and parents
of the Medical Outpatient Department at
Great Ormond Street Hospital for Children,
for generously answering her many queries.

*First published in Great Britain 2000
Harlequin Mills & Boon Limited,
Eton House, 18-24 Paradise Road, Richmond, Surrey TW9 1SR*

© Sheila Danton 2000

ISBN 0 263 82436 5

*Set in Times Roman 10½ on 11¼ pt.
112-0101-51122*

*Printed and bound in Spain
by Litografia Rosés S.A., Barcelona*

CHAPTER ONE

GAIL PETERS checked her watch. Eight-fifteen already. She took a deep breath, pushed back her shoulder-length hair and made her way into the chest clinic.

Unbolting the child-proof barrier, she smiled at the middle-aged lady who she presumed was the clinic receptionist. 'Hi. I'm your replacement SHO. Destined to be the bane of your life until I find my way around.' She bolted the low barrier behind her.

Betty smiled and said, 'Good morning, Doctor…' She peered short-sightedly at Gail's Badge. 'Dr Peters, is it?'

'Gail, please.'

'Then good morning, Gail. Welcome to the breath of fresh air that is Lizzie's chest clinic.' She chuckled proudly at her own joke which Gail guessed she repeated to every newcomer.

She leaned over and removed a long blonde hair from Gail's dark sweater. 'You don't mind, do you? You look so smart otherwise.' She lifted her eyes to Gail's hair. 'Definitely one of yours. No gossip there.'

After laughing with her for a moment, Gail asked, 'Where is everybody?'

'Ain't nobody here but me and I don't expect anyone else until nearer nine. The clinic won't start until nine-fifteen this morning. Meantime I'll give you a quick sight-seeing tour and then show you the clinic diaries.'

Having just completed her pre and post registration house jobs which had left her chronically tired from long hours and lack of sleep, Gail thought it sounded too good to be true. As Betty led the way across the gaily painted

5

waiting area, Gail asked, 'Do all the clinics start at that time?'

'Why, bless you, no. We've been all at sixes and sevens recently. What with the reg away skiing and not due back until tomorrow, then your predecessor moving on, the consultant has had to delay starting his research job in America.'

'Mr Owen hasn't left yet, then? When I spoke to him he said he was going last month.'

'Well, he has and he hasn't. He's had his leaving party but he's still helping us out. Shouldn't be for long, though. They were interviewing for the new consultant last Friday. You'll probably have to start today's clinic by yourself, though. Vic Owen's never been an early riser!'

Suddenly aware the job wasn't going to be the cushy number it had seemed a moment before, Gail asked anxiously, 'What is the clinic this morning?'

'A TB follow-up clinic.'

'Tuberculosis?' Gail frantically tried to recall what she knew about the disease.

'Shouldn't be a problem,' Betty assured her with the nonchalance of someone who didn't have to take the responsibility. 'They're all on medication and it's just to check they have no problems and ensure they're taking it regularly.'

Thankful that she'd done some reading about chest diseases over the past few days, Gail murmured, 'They'll all need blood tests and…'

'That should all have been taken care of last week. You'll find the results in the case notes. All you need do is fill in the same test requests for next month—unless there's someone you're really worried about. Those'll have to wait for Mr Owen.'

'Good morning, Betty. Scaring our new recruit half to death, are you?'

They both swung round and Betty was the first to find her voice. 'I didn't expect you yet.'

'Morning, Gail.' He grinned before telling Betty, 'As it's my last day I made a special effort. *And* I've been up to the unit already!'

'Your last day?' Betty's forehead creased worriedly, then she said, 'Oh! I see. From tomorrow Matt'll be holding the fort until the new consultant starts. Is that it?'

Vic Owen winked at Gail, before teasing, 'Yes and no.'

She frowned. 'What do you mean?'

'You mean you don't know?' His eyes held a mischievous twinkle. 'I can't believe you haven't heard.'

'Heard what?' Betty pressed eagerly. 'What should I know?' When he hesitated, she repeated, 'What have I missed?'

'Matt is your new consultant.'

Betty squealed excitedly. 'You really mean that? How wonderful. I didn't know he'd applied.' Betty edged towards the office. 'Oh! I can't wait to tell everyone.'

'I guessed as much…' Vic laughed '…so we'll leave you to it. Come through to the consulting room, Gail.' His behaviour had made clear his respect for Betty, despite her proclivity to gossip.

He closed the door behind them and lifted the first set of notes from the pile awaiting him. 'It's good to meet you in person at long last.'

Gail smiled her acknowledgement. The job at Lizzie's was a rotation post from the London hospital where Gail had trained and, as she had been the first applicant, Vic Owen had offered her the job after a brief telephone chat.

'I heard Betty telling you about this morning's clinic. It sounds straightforward enough but it has its problems. It's difficult for anyone brought up in our nanny state to comprehend that any parent would be so foolish as to risk their children's lives by not following the treatment regime we have prescribed, but I'm afraid non-compliance is a very great problem.'

'Because they don't trust the medication, or—'

'There are many reasons and, before any of us can start to deal with them, we need to understand the culture of the countries each of them have grown up in and their former way of life.'

Gail nodded. She hadn't been at medical school very long before she'd realised that the intake at the private day school she had attended was not representative of the cosmopolitan population of Britain. She had certainly learnt a lot in those early days, and felt she was a better person for it.

Vic was still telling her about the patients who would be attending that morning when there was a commotion along the corridor.

He grinned ruefully. 'I guess my successor has just arrived and as from now I am the forgotten man! I shouldn't be surprised. Betty has always mothered Matt. I guess it's because he's not married. Come on out and meet your new boss.'

Gail followed Vic into the waiting area that was now filling up with patients and was amazed that he knew them all by name. He exchanged a few pertinent words with every waiting family and it was obvious how special he made each one of them feel.

Another lesson learnt, she thought, though with only six months in post she doubted if she would match his achievement.

When they reached the reception area it was manned by a smiling nurse. 'This is Gail, your new house officer, Pam.'

'Pleased to meet you.' They shook hands.

'If you have a problem, ask Pam. There's nothing she doesn't know about this speciality or the running of the department.' He grinned conspiratorially at Pam. 'I'm about to introduce Gail to the new consultant. I guess Betty's closeted with him somewhere.'

Obviously amused, Pam raised a resigned eyebrow. 'They are in Matt's old room.'

Vic took Gail's arm. 'Come through and meet him, then we can get this clinic underway.' He pushed open an adjacent door and, laughing, asked, 'What's going on in here, then? You're setting a bad example to our new SHO.'

Gail moved forward intending to greet and congratulate the new consultant but her first glimpse of him left her speechless.

Things seemed to happen in slow motion for a few moments as she recognised he was as taken aback as she was before he finally managed to stammer out, 'G-Gail. I—I'd no idea. I thought your heart was set on becoming a lawyer.'

'It was,' she muttered. 'But thanks to you I had to change.'

She watched the disbelief spread across his face, but as he started to speak Vic took charge of the situation. 'Looks like you two have a lot to talk about. But not now. There's work to be done. Come through, Gail, and we'll see the first patient together.'

She followed him back to his room but her thoughts were anywhere but on her work. Matt Roberts. Her new consultant. It didn't bear thinking about. She would have to work closely with him for the next six months. An impossibility if she was to retain her sanity. Memories of her dead brother flooded back and she felt tears fill her eyes as she took the seat beside Mr Owen.

He rested a hand over hers and said gently, 'I don't know what has happened between you two in the past and I don't want to know. It was plain to see how shocked you both were, but in our position we can't let personal matters affect our work. Try and shelve your thoughts for the moment, Gail. It's our patients who are important for the next three hours.' He lifted his receiver and asked Betty to bring two cups of coffee through, then wheel in the first patient.

Knowing he was right, she nodded and dabbed her eyes. 'I'm OK now.'

Nevertheless, in every quiet moment, she couldn't prevent her thoughts returning to Matt and dwelling on the impossibility of the situation. Especially when she finally admitted to herself that, despite the hatred she felt for him, her traitorous body had stirred uncomfortably when she had first recognised his ruggedly classic features topped by those unruly dark curls.

Not wanting to think about it, she dragged her thoughts back to the job in hand. The first boy brought in by Pam with his mother and sister was a Yugoslavian refugee. Vic explained quietly to Gail that he had completed his treatment some three months earlier and this was hopefully his final check-up at the clinic.

Mik was five years old and his mother could speak little English so she had brought her eldest daughter to interpret.

Vic enquired about his health over the past month and was rewarded with a description of the energetic antics of a normal child.

After physically checking the boy and studying the results in his notes, Vic smiled and said to the boy's sister, 'I don't think we need to see Mik here again. He's recovered well and should have no further problems. However, if your mother is worried about him she should take him back to your GP immediately.'

The girl explained all this in their own language and their mother clasped her hands together tightly and, repeatedly bowing her head, murmured, 'Thank you. Thank you. Thank you, Doctor.'

Vic smiled and shook hands with them all as they left. 'One more satisfied customer,' he told Gail. 'Mik's family were one of the co-operative ones and he took his tablets regularly. We saw him when the disease was in the early stages, so hopefully he should have no more problems. If a relapse is going to occur, it's usually within three months of completing treatment.'

The next two had been on medication for a similar length of time, but their families had totally different attitudes to the drug regime.

The first, from South Africa, were so over-anxious that they were in danger of smothering the girl with care. It took Vic quite a long time to convince them that she was getting better.

The second, the family of a listless Asian boy, Ashok, were obviously suspicious of the drugs, claiming they were making him worse. Vic tried to make them understand that their son would be much worse if he kept missing doses, but the list was running late by the time he'd tried to convince them over and over again why the prolonged treatment was necessary.

When they eventually left, he shook his head. 'I'd better warn Matt about this one. I don't believe they have any intention of giving him the tablets. If I'm right, he'll have to be admitted, but it's a dreadful waste of a bed. I'll ask Matt to get onto his GP and ask if his treatment can be supervised by the district nursing staff.'

'If not, would he be admitted to the medical ward?'

'No, we have a small respiratory unit. Any serious emergencies are admitted to ITU or the high dependency unit, so we're there to take them when they are over the worst and to take children like Mik and the two who're there at the moment.'

'Only two—'

He anticipated Gail's query. 'One child with cystic fibrosis for IV drugs and an undiagnosed toddler in for tests which have confirmed he's also suffering from CF. He'll probably go home tomorrow. As you can imagine, the numbers in the unit fluctuate daily.'

'So are we responsible for the unit?'

He nodded. 'In conjunction with the two clinical nurse specialists, Joy and Monica who, like Pam, almost know more than you or I!'

'Certainly me!' Gail agreed. 'What about the chest patients on ITU and HDU?'

'They're in the hands of the intensive care team, but we liaise with them as necessary. It works well.'

While Gail was making notes, he rang through to Reception and when Betty told him there was no one waiting to be seen he asked for another cup of coffee. 'I think we deserve this.'

Matt joined them, bringing the tray of coffee with him.

'I didn't know this was part of your new duties,' Vic joked, then, obviously noticing the serious expression on his face, he asked, 'Problem?'

After flicking an anxious sidelong glance towards Gail, Matt explained, 'A local GP asked if we could push in a little lad he's worried about. He's three weeks old, has no history of a cold or any other infection and he isn't febrile or cyanosed, but when crying makes a horrendous noise as he breathes in.'

'Infantile larynx?' Vic enquired.

'That's what I suspect, but his parents are transferring their anxiety to him and he won't stop crying so I can't assess what he's really like at rest. I wondered if you'd take a look at him.'

'Why don't we bring him along and leave Mum and Dad with you? You can explain what you think it is while we try to quieten him and assess the degree of stridor.'

Matt gratefully accepted the offer and Gail followed him through to his room and sympathetically lifted the crying child from his mother's arms. 'I'm only taking him to see another doctor two doors away. Dr Roberts can chat to you then.'

The baby's mother watched her suspiciously. 'What are you going to do?'

'Nothing but monitor his breathing,' she told her with what she hoped was a reassuring smile, although she herself had heard nothing so horrific before.

Even as she walked back to Vic's room cradling the baby, he began to quieten; a few moments more of rocking resulted in peace descending.

Vic smiled. 'Great. No problem now he's at rest. I think we can safely confirm our diagnosis.'

'What exactly is it?' Gail asked quietly. 'And what needs to be done?'

'Infantile larynx? Sometimes called floppy larynx. It nearly always presents within the first four weeks of life and, unless it gets worse or starts to happen while the child is asleep, there's nowt to be done. Except reassure the parents that we know what we're talking about. That's the tricky part.'

'I'm not surprised,' Gail retorted. 'He sounded dreadful when I picked him up. Is there some kind of abnormality?'

Vic shook his head. 'No. It's just an exaggerated response of the airway on inspiration.'

'Will he always have it?'

'It usually disappears by the second birthday, but it is frightening, especially when the child gets a cold. We'll arrange to see him again at any time, day or night, if they are worried and definitely next week at the O and S clinic. After that we'll keep an eye on him every couple of months. If there's any change, we'll get him in for tests. Come on, we'd better return him to his mum now.'

As Gail followed him out, she asked, 'What on earth is the O and S clinic?'

Vic laughed. 'That's what we call Wednesday morning's little lot. Odds and Sods. We get a bit of everything that day. And in the afternoon we re-read the tuberculin tests that we weren't sure about on Monday.'

They walked into Matt's consulting room together and Gail sensed his eyes watching her every move. She handed the baby back to his mother, who accepted the sleeping child with relief.

'He's fine,' Vic told her. 'I expect Dr Roberts has explained why it happens.'

Mrs Jackson looked up at him vaguely and Gail could see she had been so worried about what was happening to her child that she hadn't taken in a word.

Matt started to gently explain again.

Vic ushered Gail out of the room.

'Let's finish this clinic for Matt.'

There were no problems with the remaining patients and when they'd seen the last one he said, 'I'm sure you can see already that by far the largest part of our job in paediatrics is dealing with the parents.'

Gail nodded. 'I've had very little to do with sick children up to now. With any children, really.'

He grinned. 'Your maternal instinct gives you a distinct advantage over us men. Look at the way you handled that baby. Like a natural, wasn't she, Matt?' he appealed to his colleague who had joined them.

Matt sighed. 'You can say that again. I didn't know what I was going to do. Pam was busy, the clinic assistants were missing and, though Betty's usually good with crying babies, I knew that noise would scare the wits out of her. You worked miracles, Gail.'

She raised her eyes to meet his for the first time since he had entered the room and was surprised to read a guarded admiration there. She shrugged. 'He'd probably just exhausted himself with his crying.' She rose from her seat and collected the notes together before making for the door. 'I'll take these back to Betty.'

She knew Vic was puzzled and probably more than a little worried that all his work building up the chest clinic was in danger of being destroyed by the animosity he must sense between the doctors who would be running it from the next day.

'Let him think what he likes,' she muttered to herself as she crossed the waiting area. 'It's Matt Roberts' fault I'm here and if my presence makes life difficult for him, I won't complain.'

'What was that you were saying?'

She had moved within Betty's hearing without realising it. 'Sorry,' she told a curious Betty. 'Just something I needed to get off my chest.'

Betty raised an eyebrow but didn't press for an explanation. Instead she told Gail, 'The afternoon clinic is mainly asthmatics. It starts at two.'

Gail smiled, partly in acknowledgement and partly with relief. Asthma was something she knew about. 'In that case I'll go back to my room and finish unpacking.'

'When did you move in?'

'Late last night. The previous tenant only moved out in the afternoon.'

Betty nodded her commiseration. 'The pressure on the staff accommodation is unbelievable, but it's not surprising when you see the price of what's on offer round the park.'

'Do you live there?'

Betty shook her head. 'I have a small house near the cricket ground.' A sadness shadowed her eyes. 'My Ronnie loved the game. We only moved there a couple of years before he died.'

For some reason Gail had guessed she was a widow, but hadn't liked to ask. 'I'm sorry,' she murmured.

'Knocked off his bike, he was, before all these new routes were made for cyclists. Not that they're much better!'

'I'm sorry,' she mumbled again.

'It all happened a long time ago. You go and get your unpacking done and have a bite to eat. It could be a long afternoon.'

Gail made her way through the front hall on her way to staff accommodation. Noticing the open shops, she decided to get herself a couple of apples to tide her over for the afternoon, then, noting a small rack of pre-packed sandwiches, added a pack of cottage-cheese variety to her purchases.

One or two people nodded or smiled at her as she made her way to the top floor of the staff quarters. She wondered if Matt had a room there, but decided it was unlikely, even though Vic Owen had said he was unmarried. She couldn't help wondering why. A good-looking man like him must surely have had plenty of interest from girls. Hadn't she herself had a crush on him when her brother had brought him home all those years ago?

Thank goodness he hadn't taken any notice of her at the time. She had been only fourteen when they'd first met and sixteen the last time she'd seen him, by which time her feelings for him had been totally opposite.

In fact she still couldn't think about him without the bitterness over her brother's death creeping back. A feeling she was going to have to somehow learn to ignore if they were to work together for the next six months.

And until a new registrar was appointed, it looked as if they'd be working together pretty closely.

She brushed a stray tear from her eye and started unpacking another case. It was sod's law that the photograph of her daredevil brother was on top of that box. She picked it up and stared at it, the tears flowing freely this time. 'Oh, George, I do miss you. I wish it was you I was working with. I was so looking forward to this job until Matt appeared. I knew you'd like me to specialise in chest medicine and I thought I'd enjoy working with children. Never in my wildest dreams would I have imagined Matt might do the same. It just goes to show how guilty he feels about you.'

She kissed the photograph and placed it on the bedside table. 'The next six months will not be easy for him, George. I promise.'

She was startled by the bedside telephone ringing. 'Hello?'

'Gail. It's Matt.'

He hadn't needed to tell her that. The moment he'd said her name her body had reacted as it had when she had first seen him that morning. 'Yes?'

'I think we need to clear the air. I'm just going to the canteen for lunch. Will you join me?'

'I'm unpacking and already have my lunch prepared.'

She heard him sigh. 'Gail. We have to work together whether we like it or not.'

'I don't see what *you've* got to dislike about it,' she muttered mutinously.

'I honestly had no idea you'd gone into medicine. When Vic mentioned the new SHO was Dr Peters—the name gave me a jolt, but I never even considered it might be you. Please believe me.'

Oh, she believed him all right. He wouldn't want to re-member anything about her family and she would be a constant reminder. There was no way she wanted to make things easy for him, but she had to think of the other people they'd be working with and the patients. So she would meet up with him and make it clear that, although she wouldn't jeopardise the friendly atmosphere within the clinic, her feelings towards him were a different matter. 'I must get on with a few jobs here, Dr Roberts, but I could meet you for coffee in the canteen in half an hour.'

'Gail,' she heard him plead as she replaced the receiver, 'you must call me Matt. If only for our patients' sake. You'll confuse the children if you insist on using Dr Roberts.'

She smiled grimly as she ate her sandwich and removed a few more bits and pieces from the packing case. But her heart was no longer in it, and she made her way to the canteen earlier than she had promised.

He rose to greet her. 'Coffee?'

She nodded.

When he returned with two overfull mugs, she thanked him and concentrated her gaze on the table.

'Gail…'

'I thought you were away skiing until tomorrow,' she muttered incongruously.

'I was supposed to be, then the interviews were brought forward to Friday, so I had to cut my trip short.'

'Were you with friends?' she asked.

'Yes,' he told her gently, 'I was with friends.'

'George's friends?'

He shook his head. 'George and I were friends, Gail. When it happened, we were with a party but they were acquaintances more than friends.'

Furiously she looked up and met his eyes for the first time. 'When ''it'' happened. ''It''? When George died, you mean. Are you too ashamed to say the truth?'

He looked round the room as if afraid who might be within earshot, then reached across and tried to grasp her hand. 'Please, Gail…'

She snatched her hand away and, leaving her coffee undrunk, strode out of the dining room, barely aware of the interested glances following her.

After a moment, Matt got up and followed her. What should have been the proudest day of his life was rapidly disintegrating into a black farce. He knew only too well that Gail's mother had totally and irrationally blamed him for her son's death, but he had understood her grief and had finally stopped visiting in the hope she would come to terms with what had happened when she didn't have him as a constant reminder.

It had been a wrench. For George's sake he had wanted to keep in contact, in the hopes that one day he would be able to convince both of them, especially Gail, of the truth. But in the end he had decided continued contact with him had only been making matters worse. At least where her mother had been concerned. He'd had no idea what Gail had been thinking as she'd been kept well out of his way apart from the day of the funeral and that had certainly not been the right time to approach her.

When she had agreed to meet him in the canteen, he had been relieved. They were going to have to work together for the next six months and he wanted to put the past behind them both so that they could work amicably.

The last thing he had expected was for her to immediately launch a question that led their conversation into the area he had made up his mind to avoid for the time being. Consequently he had said all the wrong things and antagonised her even further.

He made his way through to the chest clinic with a heavy heart. Hospitals were notorious hotbeds of gossip and by meeting her for a coffee he had hoped to prevent either Gail or himself being the latest victim. Vic Owen had already sussed there was some kind of a problem between them and, even though this was Vic's last day in the clinic, Matt had not confided the truth. To spare Gail's feelings, he had told himself. But her comments had shaken him, made him wonder if it was for his own benefit he wanted to keep the matter quiet.

When he walked into the clinic he was relieved to see Gail there, obviously chatting to Pam about some of the patients they were expecting that afternoon. Hopefully it was a good sign. When she'd left him in the canteen he had briefly wondered if she was about to walk out of the job and the hospital rather than face him again. Something that would certainly not have been in the best interests of her career.

As he made his way to his consulting room he smiled at them both, but it was only returned by Pam.

Finding Betty in the throes of moving all his personal

belongings along to Vic's old room, he protested, 'Vic might be using his room this afternoon.'

Betty shook her head. 'He's leaving everything to you now. Says he has no qualms about placing the department in your capable hands and he has plenty of ends to tie up before he leaves England. He's gone for lunch with Martyn Lennard and has promised to pop back and see you before he finally takes off.'

Aware that Gail was watching and listening, he groaned inwardly. Betty's intentions to accord him what she saw as his rightful status in the department must be rubbing salt into Gail's already raw emotions.

It didn't take a genius to work out that her brother could have been in the same position by now.

The clinic staff nurse came in with the notes for the afternoon list.

'Which would you like to see and which shall I allocate to Dr Peters?'

He sifted through the pile of folders and, extracting three, handed them to Pam who was hovering behind. 'She should be able to cope with these, with your help if necessary, then I'd like her to sit in with me for the remainder of the afternoon.'

'I must get on.' The staff nurse left them to their discussion.

'Thanks, Amy,' he called after her, then said to Pam, 'We can't expect Gail to know our way of going about things without first seeing one of us in action, can we?'

With a ruefully raised eyebrow Pam warned, 'It'll mean long clinics for you until we get a new registrar.'

'I know, but it's not fair to expect too much of our new SHO just because we don't have the full complement of staff.' He grinned. 'We could put her off children—and chests—for life!'

Pam sighed. 'I know the feeling.' She gave him a rueful wave and went in search of Gail.

*   *   *

Gail was checking the equipment in the room she had been allocated.

'Matt suggests you deal with these three and then sit in on his consultations for the remainder of the afternoon.'

Gail glared ferociously. 'If that's what he wants I suppose I'd better do as he says.'

Pam frowned. 'He's very easygoing. You don't need to worry about him firing impossible questions at you. He's not like that.'

'It wasn't that I was worrying about—'

'What, then?'

Not wanting to confide the real reason, Gail felt herself colouring as she sought a plausible explanation.

Pam roared with laughter and teased, 'I know. You fancy him. Well, I can tell you, you won't be the first.'

Gail retorted icily, 'Believe me, Pam, that is the very last thing I'm likely to do.'

CHAPTER TWO

AFTER a strained silence, Pam ventured tentatively, 'I was only joking, Gail. Because he's not married, you'll discover his love life is a regular topic of conversation around here.'

Conscious that her feelings towards Matt were in danger of affecting her relationship with the remainder of the staff of the department, Gail smiled weakly and tried to play down her earlier reaction. 'I should have realised that. In a few days I guess I'll be as bad as the rest of you. Does he have a regular girlfriend?'

Pam shook her head. 'Not that anyone here knows of. Before I got married last year we talked quite a lot about the cost of weddings and the horrific divorce rate and I think if there had been anybody, he'd have said.'

A tap on the door was quickly followed by Betty popping her head into the room. 'First patients are arriving.'

'I'm coming.' Pam smiled and left a thoughtful Gail to await the arrival of her first patient.

She was studying the case notes of the first little boy she was to see when her internal telephone rang.

'Hi.' It was Matt. 'Feel free to interrupt me if there's anything you want to know. It's not easy, I know, being thrown in at the deep end on your first day.'

'I'll do that. And thank you for the offer,' she told him formally, and although momentarily she wondered if being so nice to her was just another attempt to try and assuage his guilt, she knew in her heart that it was because he was a good and caring doctor who would want to support his junior staff whoever they may be. Why else would he have been appointed as the new consultant?

'Er—Matt? There is just one thing.'

'Yes.'

'Vic mentioned reading the tuberculin tests today and I—'

'We can talk about those later. Because of the interviews we didn't do any of them on Friday. If we had they'd have been at the morning clinic. So there's no problem.'

'I see. Thanks anyway.'

Her first patient was Wayne, a nine-year-old asthmatic who had been admitted to hospital some months previously with a severe attack that had panicked his mother into calling an ambulance. She was bringing him up on her own along with six other children of varied parentage, and clearly was finding it difficult to cope, so he had been kept as an in-patient for a couple of weeks in an attempt to educate him about his handling of his condition and the use of his prescribed drugs.

She smiled a welcome as he came into the room and looked in vain for his mother. 'Are you on your own, Wayne?'

He nodded. 'Our Syl dropped me off here on her way back to school.'

'How have you been since we saw you last?'

'Ace, miss. I don't think I need to come no more.'

Gail hid a smile at his mode of address. 'We'll think about that in a minute.'

She sat him down and asked about his daily routine and his medication.

When she was satisfied, she said, 'Let's have a listen to your chest now.'

He tugged at his shirt in an attempt to unbutton it.

'Not that way,' she protested. 'I'm not in that much of a hurry.' She helped him undo the buttons and, after warming her stethoscope in her hand, listened to his chest.

Pam came in while she was doing so and raised a querying eyebrow to know if Gail was all right.

'No problem there,' she told Wayne and included Pam

in the answer with a nod. 'Are you going on to school now, Wayne?

He looked sheepish. 'Nah. Not s'afternoon. I told Mum I'd go straight back home.'

Gail looked enquiringly towards Pam, who shrugged. 'We're a legitimate excuse for an afternoon off, I guess.'

Gail grinned. 'In that case, Wayne, we'll make your next visit in three months rather than one.' She knew she was on safe ground as Matt had written that suggested timescale in the case notes, providing Wayne was well at this visit.

'See ya then,' he told her cheerfully.

'I'll go with you to the appointments desk,' Pam told him, and waited for Gail to finish entering the details of his visit on his case notes before saying, 'Your next appointment, Emily, is here.'

Gail told her, 'I'll read through the notes and then give her a shout.'

Even before she saw her, Gail gathered Emily was a very different proposition. The only daughter of older parents, she was a similar age to Wayne, but she certainly would never arrive unaccompanied. Her parents were too anxious for that, and according to Vic's notes would spend anything necessary if they could get their daughter's asthma cured, which sadly wasn't possible, although it seemed to be under very much better control than when she had first been seen in the clinic.

Gail called her in, accompanied by both her father and her mother. When Gail asked Emily how she had been since her last appointment, it was her mother who answered. 'OK, but…is Dr Owen not available?'

Gail smiled reassuringly. 'He's moved to America, to do research into asthma.'

Emily's mother checked Gail's badge and was obviously disappointed by what she read there. 'Isn't there a new consultant?'

'There is, but he isn't available at the moment.'

'Can we see him later?'

'If necessary,' Gail told her gently, 'but for the moment, how about telling me how Emily's been getting on?'

Eventually she did as was suggested, finishing with a list of minor problems, none of which was affected by, or was a result of, the asthma.

'So, her asthma is well controlled, then?' Gail prompted.

'I suppose so,' Emily's mother responded hesitantly, 'but—'

'No more attacks like the one that brought her to our attention?' she persisted.

'No, no. Certainly not. Dr Owen said to bring her straight back to Casualty if that happened.'

'So the drugs she has been prescribed are doing the trick?'

Emily's father found his voice at last. 'I think we could safely say that. She's been better than I've seen her for years.'

His wife threw him an exasperated look, but Gail had the information she was looking for. 'Good. I'll just have a listen to her chest, then.'

Emily was quickly led into the attached examination room and while Gail waited, stethoscope in hand, helped to remove her top layer of clothes by her mother.

Every time Gail tried to listen, Emily's mother remembered something else she wanted to say, until in the end Gail smilingly asked if she would wait with her husband. 'I can't hear properly if there's the slightest sound,' she added sweetly, 'and I don't want to miss anything, as I'm sure you appreciate.'

When she had finished checking Emily's chest, Gail helped her re-dress.

'That sounds very good, so we'll just check your peak flow rate, Emily.'

The young girl was well used to using the meter and gave three blows in quick succession.

'Great, Emily. That was better than it's ever been by the looks of your notes. Have you kept a chart of your readings at home?'

Emily nodded and handed over the piece of paper she was clutching.

'These are very good, too,' Gail told her. 'You are obviously doing exactly what Dr Owen prescribed and the results are obvious.'

Hoping her positive assessment of the situation would prevent further demands to see the new consultant, Gail smiled and suggested to Emily's parents, 'If you've no further questions, why don't you make an appointment to see us again in three months' time? You can always change it if there's any problem that you need to discuss before that—but Emily's doing so well at the moment that I think it's most unlikely.'

She ushered them out of the room without giving them a chance to argue.

She closed the door behind them and when Pam joined her she sighed deeply. 'That was hairy.'

Pam chuckled. 'I expected them to insist on seeing Matt. You did well.'

'I hope they accept my opinion; they were clearly disappointed that I wasn't the new consultant. What they'll say when they realise Matt is Vic's replacement and was here all the time, I can't imagine!'

Pam grinned wryly. 'Could be interesting. They wouldn't see Matt last time they were here. They always insisted on seeing no one but Vic. That's why I said you'd done well.'

There was a tap on the door and Matt put his head round. 'Your last patient hasn't appeared, Gail. Come and sit in on the remainder of my consultations.' He led the way to his room and closed the door behind them. 'I don't know how on earth you managed to persuade Emily's mum to leave without seeing everyone from the hospital director down, but well done.'

Gail didn't reply but his unexpected compliment had a curiously warming effect on her, even though it wasn't warranted by any medical expertise she had exhibited.

Thankful he was already too immersed in reading the case notes of his next patient to notice the slight colour she knew was staining her cheeks, she waited for him to finish before asking, 'What's the problem with your next patient?'

He handed her the thick folder of notes and grimaced wryly. 'Ryan Walker is a moderately severe asthmatic who needs regular admission. In fact, nearly every time he gets an upper respiratory infection. Between times his asthma is well controlled, but it doesn't take much to tip him into a crisis.'

'How old is he?'

'Approaching twelve—'

'No sign of him growing out of it?'

Matt shook his head. 'His family history suggests that's unlikely.'

'I see. When was he last an in-patient?'

'Admitted three weeks ago. Discharged last week. Let's get him in, shall we?'

Gail leapt to her feet and, opening the door, called Ryan's name, then returned to her seat.

Ryan and his father came uncertainly into the room, and she could hear Ryan's wheeze. Matt must have heard the sound before they even reached the door. He moved across the room at speed and, taking Ryan's arm, led him to a chair beside the desk while greeting his father warmly.

Gail realised Matt was demonstrating that she had just made a big mistake. Not having worked with children before, she hadn't thought about greeting the boy in the waiting room and accompanying him into the consulting room, but she realised that was what she should have done if none of the clinic assistants were about to bring them in.

Wondering if Matt thought she considered herself too important to do something so menial, the colour darkened

in her cheeks and for a moment she wished herself anywhere but at Lizzie's.

Matt began to gently question the boy as to how he'd
been since he'd left the hospital. As he answered, Ryan's
anxious wheeze gradually subsided.

Gail was fascinated with Matt's handling of the boy. He
spoke quietly, his normal deep velvet voice modified to a
gently soothing tone. A tone that, as well as comforting the
over-anxious boy, was calming to Gail's fears of working
with Matt for the next six months.

Aware that his whole attention was fixed on the boy as
he spoke, she stole a glance at his face and was overwhelmed by the care and concern for his young patient that
was clearly visible there. The sight set her pulse racing as
she recognised she was still as physically attracted to him
as she had been all those years ago.

An attraction that could and must go no further. The
spectre of her brother would always stand between them.

With a sigh, she dragged her attention back to the consultation taking place. The only thing she could do for her
brother now was make a success of her career as a doctor.
As Matt was doing. She stole another look at his face and
wondered if the course of his career had also been changed
by what had happened.

Although she had thought her sigh inaudible, he must
have heard it for he swung his head sharply in her direction.

She smiled, albeit insincerely, so he said nothing, but she
knew her interruption had annoyed him and resolved never
again to let her thoughts wander to personal matters while
she was on duty. She might have to work with the person
responsible for her brother's death, but she *was* a professional and in future she would behave like one.

'You're measuring your peak flow regularly?' Matt
asked at length.

Ryan nodded and handed over a chart he had kept
at home.

'Would you like to give a blow for me now?'

Anticipating Matt's request, Gail had lifted the peak flow meter from the desk and inserted a clean mouthpiece. She handed it to Ryan.

'Thanks, Gail.' Matt sounded surprised and she guessed she deserved it after her earlier lapse of concentration.

Ryan blew into the meter three times in succession, each time showing Matt the result before resetting the pointer.

Matt noted down the results and pushed the chart and his notes in Gail's direction. 'You're performing well today, Ryan. Let's have a listen.' He indicated Ryan should go into the small examination room and remove his shirt.

Gail studied his notes closely. They showed a steadily improving result and she smiled her approval and slid the papers back to Matt.

He inclined his head indicating she should join him in physically checking the boy.

When he'd examined and listened to Ryan's chest, he let Gail listen but raised his hand to prevent her commenting on what she had heard.

'Not bad, Ryan, not bad at all,' Matt told him. 'You've tailed off your dosage of prednisolone like we said?'

Ryan nodded. 'Last dose tomorrow.'

Matt marked it on the chart. 'Fine. Keep on with your usual regime of inhaled drugs and we'll see how you do after that. Make an appointment for two weeks' time, but don't hesitate to come back next Monday if there's a problem. You're back at school, are you?'

Ryan shook his head and glanced towards his father. 'Dad's worried I might catch something else, so they're sending me work home.'

Matt's frown indicated that he didn't think that a good idea, but his response was gentle. 'I think you should start back again tomorrow.'

'What about his football?' Mr Walker asked anxiously.

'I should give that a miss until I see you next time, then

if all's still going well there's no reason why you shouldn't play again, Ryan.'

The boy shot his father a triumphant look and said, 'Thanks, Doc.'

Matt turned to the boy's father. 'Anything else you want to ask?'

He shook his head so Matt rose and escorted them to the door. 'See you in two weeks, then.'

He closed the door behind them and returned to his seat behind the desk. Gail said nothing while he scribbled in the notes, but when he closed the file she murmured the apology that was playing on her mind.

'That was thoughtless of me to leave Ryan to come into the room on his own. I'm sorry.'

He swung his chair round to look at her with surprise. 'I hadn't given it another thought.' She could see he meant it as he went on, 'Child medicine is a whole different world, Gail. I certainly don't expect you to know everything from day one.'

She smiled uncertainly. 'I'm pleased to hear it. I feel way out of my depth.'

'Are you intending to continue with paediatrics or is this just a routine house job on your way to some other speciality?'

Gail bristled instinctively. 'Why does everyone think because I'm female I'm going into General Practice?'

Clearly startled, Matt rushed to defend himself. 'I don't, and that wasn't what I was implying either. As I said this morning, I *was* surprised to learn you'd taken up medicine, but that was only because you were always so adamant you were going to be a lawyer.'

'And whose fault—?'

He was too angry now to listen to her heated accusation. 'I was only interested so that I would know best how to help you during your time here. I apologise for asking.'

He pulled the notes of the next patient roughly across the desk and opened the file.

She made a conscious effort to regain her self-control and then asked quietly, 'Who's next?'

'Jane Martin.'

Aware that her response to his innocent enquiry had deserved his rebuke, she murmured meekly, 'I'll go and find her, shall I?'

'I can ring through to Betty.'

'No need. I'll go.'

If she had to work with him until August, she might as well stop looking for hidden meaning in everything he said, and do so without making life miserable for herself or anyone else.

Jane was attending for a third follow-up following her admission with a severe bout of asthma. She had had no problems since and, after a probing chat and thorough check-up, Matt suggested there was no need for her to attend the clinic again unless her GP thought it necessary.

She went off quite happily and Matt remarked to Gail, 'I didn't suggest you listen to her chest because there was absolutely nothing to hear. But tell me, I forgot to ask earlier, did you hear anything in Ryan's?'

'Just a pronounced expiratory wheeze.'

'He never completely loses that but his asthma is usually well under control. The problems arise when it's exacerbated with an infection.'

'I should think you have several like that on your books, don't you?'

'Mmm. Not many that we see as regularly as Ryan. Mostly the admission is just a one-off occurrence—like Jane. Perhaps because they become a little blasé and don't follow their prescribed regimes, and maybe because until it has happened once they don't take care of themselves when infection strikes. They are usually far more careful after one stay with us.'

Relieved that her earlier outburst seemed to be forgotten, Gail nodded attentively for the remainder of the afternoon and she was surprised at how much she learnt.

During a lull, he took her up to the respiratory unit and introduced her to the nurse specialist on duty.

'Don't worry about us, Joy. We can manage unless you have any problems.'

She shook her head. 'None whatsoever. How's the clinic going?'

'Fine. Do you want Pam to relieve you for a tea break?'

Joy shook her head. 'We can manage.'

Matt showed Gail round the unit and introduced her to Peter and Joseph, the two patients.

Peter, the thirteen-year-old, obviously thought the world of Matt, and by the time his bleep warned them that the next patient had arrived in outpatients his handling of Peter had shown her he had a wonderful rapport with children.

He was also a good teacher and, without a doubt, a more than competent consultant and as the clinic came to an end, later than expected, her respect and admiration for his work conflicted with her personal feelings. As he collected the notes together to take along to Betty, he turned to her with a smile. 'George would be very proud of you.'

His voice was quiet and she knew he meant it as a compliment, but his mention of her brother was too much after the long, emotionally charged day and her struggles with the unfamiliar routine.

She felt tears pricking behind her eyes and had to get away. She leapt to her feet and placed her chair against the wall so that he couldn't see her face. 'I must get on with my unpacking.'

She sensed, rather than heard, that he was moving towards her and she tried to escape, but he grasped her arm gently and said, 'You're exhausted. Do only what's essential and then meet me later for a meal. I'll pick you up about seven.'

She was incensed at his arrogant assumption that she would even consider going out with him. 'I'm perfectly capable of finding myself something to eat, thanks.'

She could sense his exasperation and knew he was trying to find a way to break down the barrier she and her family had erected against him at the time of George's death, but, although she was now willing to work towards a cordial working relationship, she wanted nothing more from him and intended to make that clear from the outset.

'Gail, please, as I said earlier, we have to work together—'

'I'm quite prepared to do so amicably, Matt, but that's as far as it goes. Now, please let go of my arm. I have a lot to do.'

He did as she asked and she sped from the department, pausing only to ask Betty what time she was needed next morning.

'Eight forty-five OK?'

'Fine.' She knew Betty was watching her curiously, and cursed the feminine emotions that prevented her keeping a stiff upper lip. Blinded with tears, she made her way to her room and threw herself onto the bed.

'Oh, George,' she sobbed. 'How am I going to survive this nightmare? I only chose this speciality because I knew it was what you had intended. I thought adult chest problems would remind me too much of what happened to Dad, and really believed I would like working with children.

'This is the last speciality I would have envisaged Matt considering. Not enough kudos, I would have thought. I thought you told me he was going to be a surgeon. The greatest wielder of a knife that ever lived was what you said. I've always imagined him glorying in such a prestigious position.'

Her sobs stopped suddenly and she sat up, brushing away her tears as she thought about what she had just said. The Matt she'd met today was nothing like that. Had she been mistaken all those years ago, or had Matt changed? If so, was it because of the burden of guilt he was carrying?

Matt watched her race out of the department and shook his head ruefully.

Betty took the notes from his hands and asked, 'What on earth have you said to her?'

Determined not to give Betty anything to gossip about, he forced himself to smile. 'I was trying to compliment her on her work, but I think she's so exhausted that she took it the wrong way. I'm sure she'll be a great asset to the department so I must be careful how I phrase my words in future.'

He made his way down to the car park, his thoughts dwelling on Gail as she had used to be when he'd first gone to her home with her brother, George. Gail at fourteen. Who had believed he could do no wrong. He'd known it, even enjoyed her teenage adulation, but seven years at that time had been an enormous difference in age.

It could be very different now. If only he and George hadn't gone on that fateful French skiing holiday. George had always been the more adventurous and he'd followed where George had led.

But not that day. He had known there was a warning not to ski off-piste and had told George so, but George had been headstrong and perhaps more immature than Matt, who had been beginning to assume the responsibility necessary for his future in medicine.

George had refused to listen and when Matt wouldn't join him, he'd gone without him. Matt had believed George would give up the idea if he'd refused, but another holiday-maker, as foolhardy as George himself, had jumped at the chance to go with him.

If only he'd followed immediately! Would he have been in time to save his friend? Or would he have died himself?

In the past ten years he'd relived the events of that day

over and over again. He couldn't forgive himself for the few moments he'd allowed to elapse before deciding to go after his friend. If only to try and prevent him attempting anything even more outrageous.

If he'd been there a couple of moments earlier, perhaps he could have saved them both. He'd had the resuscitation skills necessary. But they would have been of no use if he, too, had been buried by the small avalanche.

He could never know the truth of what might have happened, but in the dark hours of the night it didn't prevent him trying.

He sighed and pulled into the parking space allocated for his luxury flat, wondering what exciting ingredients Mrs Crew, his housekeeper, had left for him to cook that evening.

Aware that, however much Matt now regretted what had happened, there was no way she could ever forgive him, Gail knew she had done the right thing by refusing to eat with him.

To do her job conscientiously, as she intended, they would have to talk about the patients. She would be pleasant and polite on those occasions. But nothing more. Just because they were working together was no reason for them to socialise—either between clinics or when off duty. The six months would soon pass and after that—with luck—their paths would never cross again.

Having made that resolve she felt very much better and resumed her unpacking.

It was late by the time she had her room in some semblance of order and she decided to reheat a can of soup for her supper.

When her empty stomach caused her to toss and turn from the early hours of the morning, she recognised she should have eaten something more. One sandwich at lunchtime and a tin of soup had not filled the emptiness in her stomach which was partly her emotional response to the situation she'd found herself in.

She was up early and arrived in the department long before the time Betty had specified. There was no one about and she wandered aimlessly round the department, trying to familiarise herself with the contents of each of the rooms Betty had pointed out the day before.

As she crossed the waiting area, she spotted an Action Man doll, balanced precariously on the top of a pot plant where a child must have hidden it the day before. She lifted it down, intending to replace it in the toy box and then, surprised by how supple the joints were, she sat down on the nearest child-size chair and moved its joints first this way and that.

She smiled at the memory of her brother playing with his Action Man, very simple compared to this one. When she heard a door open, she sprang up and thrust the doll away from her. She was too late. Matt was standing at the departmental entrance.

'Broody?' he enquired jokingly.

She tried not to meet his eyes but she couldn't miss the amusement there.

'George had one of the early ones. I was interested to discover how they have developed,' she told him coldly.

She tried to push past him, but he didn't move. 'I had one as well,' he told her quietly.

When she didn't answer, he asked, 'Do you think I don't miss George too?'

She regarded him steadily. 'I'm sure you must. If you'd kindly let me pass now, I believe Betty has just arrived.'

She could see her reply had unsettled him and felt a flash of satisfaction. Surely he realised by now that the situation they found themselves in was all his fault. If George were still alive, she would have studied law as had always been her ambition. She had only taken up medicine to satisfy her mother's ambition, and, however much she was now enjoying her career, she still nursed a smouldering resentment that it wasn't the one she had chosen for herself.

He let her pass, but didn't follow. Instead, she noted from the corner of her eye, he picked up the Action Man and examined it thoughtfully.

CHAPTER THREE

'IT's the CF clinic this morning,' Betty greeted her.

Gail nodded. 'I saw the sign you'd put up last night. I suppose you have a large number of children with cystic fibrosis?'

'Enough for clinics twice a week. Day-long clinics at that.'

'What time do they start?'

'The day cases come at nine.'

'Day cases? How many?'

'Three. That's really all we've room for.'

'That explains the cubicled room in the bottom corner.'

'That's the one.' She handed Gail three sets of notes. 'They start off with Pam in her room. You can take a look and then leave them in there for her. She'll call you if she needs help.'

She was still in the day room perusing the three sets of notes when Matt came in search of her. She looked up enquiringly.

'Have you a moment, Gail?'

She nodded warily.

'Have you had much experience with children with cystic fibrosis?'

She shook her head. 'I'm afraid not. This is my first time with paeds.'

He nodded. 'In that case, perhaps you'd prefer to sit in on my consultations. These children have specific needs, but they are pretty similar, so once you get used to the routine—'

'I appreciate that. I'm sorry I'm not more use to you.'

'Believe me, Gail, you're much more use to me admitting your lack of knowledge on the subject, than if you pretend you know what you are doing and consequently make mistakes.'

'Until you get a registrar it means a long clinic for you. That's the only problem.'

He smiled warmly. 'You'll learn enough to be a great help long before we find a replacement reg. After only one day of working with you I'm confident of that.'

His compliment uncontrollably stimulated the nerve-endings in her skin into a pleasant warmth, but, having determined to keep any contact between them on a purely work-orientated basis, she tried to ignore it, and asked briskly, 'When do you expect your first patient?'

An exasperated quirk of his eyebrow told her he had hoped his compliment would result in a thawing of her attitude, but, clearly recognising that wasn't on the cards, he didn't pursue it. 'My first patient is at nine. An eight-year-old who was referred to us last week for diagnosis after increasingly severe chest infections. Nothing else significant—she doesn't exactly look well-nourished, but that could be put down to her background, and there is a suggestion that she has more bowel movements than is normal each day.'

'Has she any family history?'

He smiled. 'She's in care. Abandoned several years ago. Nothing known about her family and she has been placed, fairly unsuccessfully, with several families to date.

'She had a new placement a couple of months ago. Her new foster mum was soon concerned at the repeated infections and it was their GP's decision to check her out.'

'And?'

'I'm afraid it looks a positive diagnosis.'

'Poor girl. She's got everything stacked against her, hasn't she?'

'Yes and no. If it's only recently become a problem, her lungs may not be too badly damaged and the X-ray we took last week looks hopeful. But how long she's been having these infections is something else we don't really know. Her most recent GP has been trying to find some earlier records for her, but so far without success.'

'So where do you go from here?'

'Intensive physio training and dietetic advice for a start. As her chest was clear last week, I think we need to do regular culture of her sputum *and* immediately she contracts another infection.'

'Do you have a dedicated physio?'

'Jackie. She'll be with us today.'

Pam joined them as he answered her last question.

'And she'll soon be looking for her first day patient, so I need to get started.'

Matt jokingly touched an imaginary forelock. 'Yes, ma'am.'

He led the way to his own consulting room where the notes of Emma, the young girl they'd been discussing, were on his desk.

He opened them and checked the various results. 'Hmm. These suggest she is not absorbing her food as well as she should either, so she needs to start on enzyme supplements with her meals right away.'

'And vitamins?'

Once again he seemed impressed by the knowledge she had gleaned from her textbooks only a couple of days before. 'That goes without saying.'

When she joined them with Mrs Grange, her foster mother, Matt asked, 'Do you remember me—Matt? And this is Gail.'

Emma was not an easy child to deal with. She ignored what he was saying and behaved more like a bolshie teenager, which wasn't altogether surprising considering her life to date. She clearly resented being there and blamed her foster mother, whom she called Ma, for initiating the investigations.

Every time Matt tried to tell Mrs Grange what was going to be necessary to help Emma, the little girl piped up, 'You'd better tell me. She's not my mother. It'll be someone else next week.'

Gail's heart went out to the little girl, who'd already suffered more than she should have to cope with at her age, and wished she could find some way to help her to accept what they were doing was all for the best.

Matt clearly felt the same as he chided gently, 'You know, Emma, we can do a lot to keep you well, but we need your help too.'

The little girl shrugged and looked down at the floor. Gail sensed her misery and isolation and wished she could give her just some of the cuddles missing from her short life, but she knew that wasn't a viable option. However, it was clear Matt needed space to talk to Mrs Grange and she suggested instead, 'Have you seen our tropical fish?'

Emma nodded but stubbornly refused to look at Gail.

'I'm new here and keep meaning to go and have a look at them. Why don't we go together and you can tell me what you know about them?'

After a moment's hesitation, Emma glowered first at Matt and then at Mrs Grange, then muttered aggressively, 'What d'ya wanna know?'

Gail heard Matt sigh with relief at the minor victory she had scored, but she had no idea how she was going to follow it up. 'Anything you can tell me,' she told Emma as she closed the consulting-room door behind them. 'How many fish do you think there are in the tank?'

She had searched for a question that the little girl would be able to make a stab at answering. Her confidence desperately needed the boost of knowing something more than these know-all adults.

'Thousands,' Emma boasted. 'I counted loads of babies last week.'

They couldn't get very close as a couple of slightly older

boys had moved chairs in front of the tank and were kneeling on them.

Emma shoved the first one off his chair and he ran to his mother. 'You too,' she threatened the other one, 'and take the chairs with you. I have to show this doctor the fish,' she told him importantly.

Gail felt she couldn't let Emma get away with behaving in that way, but she had to do it without alienating the girl before she had even begun to trust her. 'That wasn't very kind, Emma. I wouldn't have minded waiting until they had finished looking at the fish,' she said gently. 'I don't expect they like being here any more than you do. And boys aren't as brave as girls.'

Gail watched Emma glance back at the boys before saying, 'They're bigger than me.'

'Maybe, but they're probably just as scared.' She held her breath for a moment, wondering if Emma would deny the suggestion, but breathed with relief when the girl jabbed a finger at the glass and said, 'Look at that one. It's enormous.'

They chatted about the fish for a little while longer and then Emma became bored and started back towards Matt's room. 'I'm going home now.'

'Let's put the chairs back for the boys, shall we?' Emma watched as Gail did so and smiled at the boys, but she made no attempt to help.

Gail didn't comment, but took Emma's hand and walked across the room and tapped on Matt's door.

When she opened it a crack, he beckoned them in and his initial greeting was accompanied by an approving smile when he saw Emma already trusted her sufficiently to hold her hand.

'Come and sit down, Emma.' As he spoke he moved Gail's chair nearer to Emma's.

'I'm going home now.' Emma was petulant.

'We'd like you to stay with us a little longer today.'

'I don't want to. I'm hungry.'

Gail smiled. 'That's no problem. We can find you a snack now *and* some lunch if you're still here.'

Emma wrinkled her nose in a sniff then wiped the back of her hand across it. 'Why do I have to stay?'

'Now we know why you keep getting these chesty coughs, we want you to learn how to stop them happening again—'

'I wanna go home.' She started to cry.

Gail reached across and took hold of her hand.

'I'll be here and I need to learn all these things as well.' She flashed a look of appeal at Matt and breathed a sigh of relief when she saw he had grasped what she was trying to suggest.

'I've just had a good idea, Emma. Perhaps you and Gail can find out together what you both need to know.'

Emma looked suspiciously from one to the other, then at her foster mother again. 'You staying?'

'For a little while. I have to get back to give Jeremy his lunch, but I'll be back this afternoon.' Mrs Grange had a seven-year-old son of her own.

Emma turned to Gail. 'You got a bad cough as well?'

Gail shook her head. 'No, but, like I said, I'm new here and I have a lot to learn.'

'You'll stay with me *all* the time?'

Gail raised a querying eyebrow towards Matt.

'Maybe not quite every minute, but she'll see you aren't left on your own. Just for a moment, though, I want a quick word with her about someone else, so if you and your—er—mum would like to go and have another look at the fish, we'll find you a snack first.'

'She's not my mum,' Emma muttered as she made her way to the door.

The moment it had closed behind them, Gail said, 'I hardly know a soul in the department.'

He'd obviously buzzed Pam as she came in at that moment.

'Pam, can you do lung-function tests on Emma and show Gail the ropes, then introduce her to Jackie? And everyone else they both need to know?'

Pam nodded. 'Anything else?'

'First organise a mid-morning snack for Emma. And some lunch.' He laughed. 'She's apparently starving. While you're doing that it'll give me a chance to have a word with Gail.'

When Pam had gone he chuckled. 'By the end of today, you'll know this department better than I do. I was going to suggest you sat in with the physio and the dietitian later, but this is as good a time as any. That little girl needs all the support we can give her. You did well to gain her confidence so quickly.'

'Mmm. I should think she's been ignored for so long that she'll take to anyone who shows the slightest interest in her.'

'That could be dangerous.'

'I think she can probably take care of herself. You should have seen how she dealt with two bigger boys who were in her way.'

'Let's hope so. Now, Jackie saw her last week, but according to her foster mum Emma has ignored all she was told. So I want her to see her again *and* the dietitian, Lisa. I guess she won't like that either, but I've asked them both to try and impress on her the need to comply. Perhaps you can help.'

Gail nodded. 'What about the clinic?'

'You can sit in with me this afternoon. Emma should be able to go home by mid-afternoon at the latest. Have you done any spirometry?'

'A long time ago.'

'It won't do you any harm to watch Pam, then. We usually have a technician to do the respiratory function tests, but he's away on a course.'

Gail felt herself dismissed and went in search of Pam. For a brief moment she wondered if he hadn't wanted her sitting in with him all day, but decided he was doing it for everyone's sake. As well as Emma needing support, the sooner she could see some of the patients herself, the better it would be for him, but first she needed to learn what each member of the chest clinic team did.

When lunch-time arrived Gail couldn't believe the morning was gone already. She had learnt a lot and had certainly enjoyed herself. Every member of the clinic staff had been kindness itself to Emma and Gail, and Matt's appointment as consultant seemed universally popular.

'He's such an easy person to work with,' Lisa told her, obviously smitten by Matt's charm. 'He's the most sought-after bachelor in the hospital, but he doesn't seem to notice. He gets loads of invitations but he rarely accepts one. It's as if he's made a conscious decision not to get involved. At least with anyone from the hospital.'

Not wanting to add to any gossip, Gail said jokingly, 'I don't blame him. By the sound of things it would cause a riot if he did.'

Lisa laughed. 'When you get to know him better, I bet you'll feel the same way about him.'

I bet I won't, Gail thought, but changed the subject to ask about the need for high-energy foods Lisa had tried to impress on Emma. 'I thought she'd be over the moon at being told to eat things like fish and chips and high-calorie snacks between meals but she wasn't at all impressed, was she?'

'The trouble is we haven't a clue what her diet has been like in the past. It could just be a poor diet that's the problem, or perhaps she's unconsciously rejected the foods that upset her tummy.'

'I guess so.'

'Unfortunately they very often don't feel like eating much of the time. But once they realise they feel so much better if they do what we suggest, they do try. Not that they don't try and cheat now and again, but that doesn't hurt unless they keep doing it.'

They walked over to the day room where Emma, another girl and two boys were tucking into a chicken dinner.

Seeing Emma happily chatting to the others, Gail left her to it and went to see if Matt required any help.

He was writing in the notes of the youngster he had seen at the end of his morning list.

'How's it going?' he asked.

'Fine. Emma's eating lunch with a new-found friend.'

'She's started on her enzymes and vitamins?'

Gail nodded. 'And because the others took them, she's taken them today without a murmur. Doesn't want to look a wimp, I guess.'

'I'm just going to pop up to the unit and see one of our older CF boys. His GP thinks his chest infection needs more than the usual home treatment. Do you want to come up?'

Gail nodded. 'Please.'

Gail followed Matt into the unit. Joy handed him a set of notes saying, 'He's nebulising at the moment.'

'With antibiotics?'

'For two days but he's deteriorating.'

'Sputum culture?'

She handed him the GP's letter.

Matt nodded. 'Let's have a look at him.' He passed the case notes to Gail and indicated she should go with them.

'Hi, Robin. What are you doing here?'

A pale-faced boy who looked younger than his thirteen years removed his nebuliser mask and tried to grin. 'It's starting to spit.' He indicated that his mother should switch off the machine.

'Let's have a listen.' Matt placed his stethoscope at various sites on Robin's chest, then indicated Gail should listen too. When she stood back, he asked, 'X-rays?'

Joy produced the films and he examined them closely.

'I think we'll start IV drugs immediately.' He turned to Robin's mother and checked the information documented in the boy's notes. 'No allergies that you know of?'

'That's right. He's never had a reaction to any to my knowledge.'

Matt nodded and carefully calculated the dosage required before turning to Gail and asking, 'Would you like me to do it?'

She shook her head. Even if she needed to be told which drug, this was something she could do.

Matt remained nearby chatting to Peter and his mother, then to Joseph's Dad.

When she had finished and Joy had helped her to make Robin comfortable, Matt nodded his approval. 'Seems like you're pretty nifty with a needle. Are you coming to the canteen for lunch?'

'I have a sandwich waiting in my room.' After his generous compliment she was as surprised as he was by her automatically defensive response, especially as she hadn't bothered to stock up with food. However, she knew she could always pick up a sandwich at the shop.

He appeared puzzled. 'The meals in the canteen are very good value.'

'I can imagine, but I have things I want to do.' She made her way through the front hall to the shop and on across the courtyard to the staff flatlets, but not without a pang of regret. A cooked meal would have gone down very well.

But she was grateful to her subconscious mind for prompting the spontaneous refusal. For there was no doubt about it, she liked him too much. After only one and a half days working with him, not only was her professional respect for him growing by the minute, but the physical attraction he held for her was as great, if not more so, as it had been all those years ago. Something she was determined to suppress at all costs.

She gave an involuntary shudder as she switched on the kettle in her room and threw herself on the bed muttering, 'If only…if only…'

'If only what?' she demanded of herself. 'You know perfectly well that if George was still alive he'd probably be working in a hospital at the other side of the country from Matt and you'd be practising law somewhere else again. Your paths would never have crossed and you would not have given him another thought.'

With her own admonishment ringing in her ears, she made a mug of coffee, unwrapped her sandwich and resolutely tried to ignore thoughts of Matt.

Half an hour later she made her way back to the clinic looking forward to sitting in with Matt for the whole of his afternoon list. Especially as he was seeing Emma again before the first appointment.

She smiled at the girl as she came into the room with her foster mother, who had not long returned from feeding her son his lunch.

'So how do you feel about things now, Emma?' Matt greeted her with a grin. 'We're not so bad as you thought, are we?'

The girl twisted her nose in a sniff. 'Don't like that coughing everything up.'

'No one does, but it's probably the most important part of keeping you fit from now on.'

Another twist of the nose. 'Suppose. Bet you've never tried it.'

Gail hid a laugh, but not quickly enough to prevent Matt noticing. 'That's where you're wrong, Emma, and you too.' He nodded towards Gail. 'I try to experience as many of the things I put my patients through as I can. So there,' he added childishly, much to Emma's delight and Gail's surprise.

'Come and see us again in a couple of weeks, Emma,

and if you've done all you've been told you should feel a whole lot better by that time.'

The remainder of the afternoon's list was an anticlimax. When they broke for a cup of tea brought in by Pam, Matt said, 'We could do with a few more characters like Emma to liven the place up, couldn't we?'

Gail shook her head. 'One's enough for me at the moment. I'm enjoying this afternoon just because it's so relaxed and peaceful.'

A statement she regretted making when Matt was seeing his last patient and she took the tea tray back to the clinic kitchen.

She hadn't noticed anything amiss until she saw Betty standing rigid behind her desk and trying to nod towards something behind Gail, without being seen.

Something made her turn round slowly rather than spinning on her heels as she would normally have done. She found herself looking into the barrel of a shotgun pointed in Betty's direction.

'Where is he?' the man asked.

'Wh-who?' Gail stammered.

'The top guy. The one who killed my daughter.'

Gail felt an icy hand clutch at her heart. Was he talking about Vic or Matt? And what did he mean, killed his daughter? Surely, surely not—she swallowed hard—surely Matt hadn't been responsible for someone else's death?

Her eyes wide, she said quietly, 'I—I don't know who or what y-you're talking about, but can't you put that down while we discuss it?'

'She knows.' He indicated Betty with a wave of the gun. 'Ask her.'

'Matt persuaded his wife to let their daughter have a transplant operation,' Betty gabbled, 'and she died, so he wants to see Matt.'

Gail moved very slowly to seat herself near the fish tank and patted the seat of the chair a couple of spaces away.

'Dr Roberts is busy at the moment. Come and sit down until he's free, Mr…?'

'Mr Bertoli,' Betty supplied as she tried to edge out of sight.

The gunman glared wildly at Gail. 'I want to see him. *Now.*'

Gail's thoughts swung crazily. 'He's seeing a patient. A little girl. She's ill. Like your little girl was. You would hate yourself if you upset her, wouldn't you?'

Mr Bertoli's face crumpled, he dropped the gun to the floor, then sank onto the chair. He covered his face with his hands and she could hear his muffled cry, 'Oh, God. Oh, God.'

Gail moved closer and placed an arm around his shoulders, at the same time kicking the weapon way out of reach of either of them. At the same moment, a couple of the hospital security men raced into the department.

They rushed over and were about to grab Mr Bertoli when Gail stopped them with a raised hand. 'Take the gun.'

They did as she said and one of them told her, 'It's not loaded. I'll call the police?'

She could feel the shudders convulsing the body of the now sobbing man and she felt an overwhelming empathy with him. He was devastated by the loss of his daughter and needed to blame somebody. And that somebody was Matt, who had suggested the transplant in the first place.

She remembered her mother ranting about wanting to kill Matt for months after her brother had died, and how she had begun to feel the same. And yet neither of them would have really tried to kill him. Neither had Mr Bertoli. He hadn't loaded the shotgun, just wanted to frighten Matt, she supposed.

'That won't be necessary.'

The security man clearly wasn't happy about that. 'I think we should—'

'No,' Gail ordered sharply. 'I'll take the responsibility.'

She looked up and saw a crowd gathered round them and knew the gunman needed privacy and to talk. Who better for him to talk to than someone like herself who had been through something similar?

She looked up at Pam and said softly, 'Help me take him across to the empty consulting room.'

Pam did so, but when Gail indicated she should leave them and close the door she protested quietly, 'Do you think that's wise?'

When Gail nodded, she pointed to the panic button under the desk and reluctantly left. As she reached the door, Gail asked, 'Would you mind bringing us a couple of coffees?'

When Pam brought the coffees, Gail could see Matt hovering just beyond the open door and guessed he had been told what had happened. She signalled to him to go away, then, when the door was closed, touched the still sobbing man on the shoulder.

'Coffee, Mr Bertoli?'

He looked up as if surprised and then took the cup with a shaking hand. 'I'm sorry. I'm sorry—I—I just didn't know what to do. I—I...' He broke off and shook his head, the tears flowing faster than ever.

Gail pulled her chair round beside him and rested her hand on his arm. 'I've only recently started here so I didn't know your daughter, but I understand exactly what you're going through because I've been there.'

He looked up at her. 'You—you lost a child?'

'A brother. But I felt just as you do at the moment.'

He gave a final juddering sob before pulling himself upright and drinking his coffee. When he'd finished, he said, 'What a bloody foolish thing—did you do anything so stupid?'

Gail shook her head. 'I was only a teenager.'

'I don't know what came over me—I've just made matters worse. I suppose they'll hand me over to the police now.'

'Would you like to tell me about your daughter? What was her name?'

'Francesca. She was beautiful.' He launched into his memories of his daughter and Gail knew she was in for a long session.

Matt paced up and down in the quiet waiting room. Everyone had left the clinic building but Pam and Betty, *and* one security man. 'I can't leave her with him. Anything could happen.'

Pam shook her head. 'I don't think you should go in, Matt. She knows where the panic button is.'

'But—'

'He probably had no intention of hurting anyone and just needs time to talk. After all, the gun wasn't loaded, was it?'

Matt took the dead girl's notes from Betty who had been across to Records to find them. 'Mmm. I thought I remembered rightly. He left her mother to cope with Francesca for eight years, only returning to the scene when he heard about the transplant. How dare he pretend he cared anything for her?'

Pam took Matt's arm and sat him down. 'You're getting as steamed up as he was, and that won't do anybody any good.'

Matt looked at her. 'I hear what you're saying but this is Gail's second day here. It has nothing to do with her. If—' He broke off and thought for a moment, then said, 'I'll ring her instead. He *has* to know there's someone around out here. And you two must go,' he added. 'It's way past time you were both home.'

'We can't leave you on your own, Matt.'

'Tom'll stay here with me, won't you?'

The security man nodded. 'But I've seen his type before. All bluster and no bottle. He shouldn't give any more trouble.'

Matt rang Gail's extension number and when she answered he almost snapped, 'OK in there?'

'We're fine.' He heard her voice with relief. It was firm and calm and held no trace of fear.

'Need any help?'

'No. We're just talking.' She replaced her receiver before he could ask anything else.

He shrugged and insisted Betty and Pam should get off duty.

He and Tom sat in silence for the next twenty minutes. 'How long do you think this is likely to go on?' the security man asked. 'It's time for my supper break.'

Matt sighed. 'I wish I knew.'

At that moment, Gail opened the door and walked across to where they were sitting.

'Mr Bertoli is going home now. There's no problem with that, is there?'

'Not if you say so,' Tom told her.

'I thought he wanted to talk with me?' Matt demanded gruffly.

'Not tonight—'

'Isn't that what he came for? To confront me—'

Gail raised a pacifying hand. 'He's changed his mind, so, if you don't mind, I suggest you disappear into your room until he's left the premises.'

Matt wasn't sure if he did mind or not. While sitting there with nothing more to do than re-read through the notes, he'd longed to remind the man about his neglect of his wife and daughter over the years. But after a moment's hesitation, he set off to do as she advised.

'What about the shotgun?' the security man asked.

'He apparently does have a licence for it, but he doesn't want it, at the moment anyway. I suggest you lock it away safely for the time being.'

'Not me! I'll hand it over to the boss. Jock can decided what's to be done with it.'

Gail frowned at Matt. 'Jock?'

'Head of hospital security.'

She nodded, clearly relieved to learn that the weapon wouldn't be her responsibility.

As he made his way into his consulting room, Matt marvelled at her calmness. It must have been a horrific situation and here she was calmly discussing the gun that had been pointed at Betty as if it were nothing more than a toy.

When Mr Bertoli had left the premises and the doors were secured, Tom left to go to the canteen. As Matt walked to where Gail was sitting, her head in her hands, he saw her shoulders were shaking. He rested a hand lightly on her shoulder. 'Are you all right, Gail?'

She rose unsteadily to her feet and he saw her whole body was shaking. 'Just reaction, I guess.'

He took her in his arms. 'You little fool. Why didn't you let the police deal with him?'

'He didn't need that on top of his loss.'

'He didn't care about his daughter, Gail. He left her and her mother to cope for eight years. *Eight* years! And he dares to pretend he cares. Guilty conscience, more like.'

'You should know,' she retorted.

'You don't leave someone you care about all that time, especially when they're ill.'

'You don't know why he left any more than he understands why you recommended a transplant might help. That's the trouble with you men. You act first and think later. He's full of regret now for what he did.'

'Huh!' Matt was as angry as Gail now. 'I'm darn sure I wouldn't walk out on someone who needed me—'

Gail picked up her jacket and, making for the exit, said darkly, 'Funny. I understood that's exactly what you did do.' She banged the door behind her, leaving Matt stunned by her accusation.

*   *   *

Gail walked unsteadily towards the staff quarters, annoyed with herself for stooping so low. But his apparent lack of understanding had infuriated her.

If only there were someone she could talk to herself as Mr Bertoli had unburdened himself to her. But she had been at the hospital too short a time to make many close friends. Pam would have been the ideal person, but Gail had no idea where she lived.

Crossing the courtyard to her flat, she was surprised to find how bitterly cold it had turned. She shivered and wrapped her jacket more closely around her, but the freezing wind, so cold it must be coming from the Arctic, managed to find a way through every seam. She looked up at the sky. Despite the cold, there was a lot of cloud about and she briefly wondered if they were about to have more snow. Traces of the last lot were still evident on unfrequented pathways, the dirty slush frozen into a hazard for the unsuspecting.

The weather was the last thing she thought about a moment later when she heard quickening footsteps behind her. As she turned to face her pursuer, it flashed through her mind that she had been a fool not to hand Mr Bertoli over to the police.

Then she saw it was Matt. And he must have seen her fear. 'I didn't give you a fright, did I?'

'What do you think?' She turned and continued on her journey. She was having difficulty in controlling her voice and just wanted to get to her room and away from him.

'I was worried about you and wanted to make sure you were all right after you stormed out. But I couldn't come after you immediately and leave the department unlocked.'

'I was fine until you scared the living daylights out of me,' she snapped.

'I'm sorry. Perhaps you'd let me take you out to dinner to make up for it. You've had one hell of an evening.'

'You're right, it's been a nightmare. And one which I

don't want to continue. I'll see you in the clinic tomorrow morning, Matt. Goodnight.'

She pressed the security numbers on the door panel and slammed the door behind her, determined he wasn't going to see the tears pouring down her face. Because she had no idea why she was crying—whether they were tears of loss, of reaction to her earlier terror, or tears because there was no way she could accept the invitation of the man she had loved since she was a gauche schoolgirl. Or at least thought she had.

CHAPTER FOUR

DESPONDENTLY Matt surveyed the closed door. He'd made a mess of that. And how! He'd been so worried about Gail's safety that he hadn't given a lot of thought to Mr Bertoli's problems.

When he'd learnt what had happened while he'd been with his last patient, and that Gail had been closeted in her room with the gunman, all he'd been able to think about was how he could lessen the perilous situation she'd been in.

She was young, inexperienced and, since her brother had died, the apple of her mother's eye. Even if she had been a stranger to him, the thought of explaining to Mrs Peters that he had stood by and allowed something to happen to her only other child was not to be contemplated.

But Gail wasn't a stranger, far from it. As he had found out in that moment of danger, he cared about her. And more than he would have believed when, as a young student, he had followed George's example and treated her like a child who should be ignored.

Even in those days he would have loved to spend more time with her. She had amused and delighted him when he had had the chance to talk to her, but George had dismissed her as an irrelevant nuisance and he had stupidly allowed his friend to drag him away.

Having no brothers or sisters of his own, he supposed he had accepted that was the way all families behaved. It wasn't until two years later that he'd recognised how wrong he had been. But by that time George had been dead and he'd been allowed no further contact with her.

Discovering she was his new house officer on the day

he'd been promoted to consultant had seemed like the icing on his cake, especially when he'd recognised how competent she was at her work.

But she had soon made it clear his delight wasn't reciprocated. And why had she just accused him of walking away when he'd been needed? She couldn't surely be talking about her mother. Mrs Peters had made it only too plain he'd been the last person she'd needed. So she must have been talking about her brother. Which meant she believed exactly what her mother did about the incident.

He sighed and checked his mobile phone was switched on, then made his way back to the car park and another lonely meal, part prepared by Mrs Crew.

Gail made her way to her room with an idea half forming in her mind. Matt had told her that morning that for the time being he didn't want her to do any on-call duty. As well as continuing the registrar's second-in-line duties, he would take over her out-of-hours rota for the next couple of weeks. He'd emphasised that it wasn't because he didn't trust her, but that he didn't think it was fair for her to have to cope with emergencies until she knew more about the speciality. So, she could get right away for the night.

She needed to talk. To unburden herself to someone who would understand the position she was in. Someone who knew what had happened all those years ago.

Who better than her mother? While Gail knew her advice wouldn't exactly be dispassionate, it was the opportunity she needed to tell her mother about Matt's reappearance on the scene.

She checked her watch and, deciding she could be there by nine, she threw a nightdress and clean undies into her overnight bag and, having ascertained her mother was going to be in, set out for Cricklewood.

Mrs Peters was overjoyed to see her. 'I didn't expect you to visit this week. Come on in and tell me all about

Lizzie's. Do you like working with children? Are you working with friendly people? Can I get you something to drink? Or to eat?'

'Whoa, Mum,' Gail pleaded, slinging her woollen jacket over a chair. 'I can't answer all those questions at once.'

'Coffee, then. And a snack?'

'That would be fantastic,' Gail told her.

'Come through and talk to me while I make it,' her mother said. 'I'm dying to hear everything.'

She primed the coffee-maker and switched it on. Gail perched on a kitchen stool, wishing, not for the first time, that her mother would make more of a life for herself, instead of trying to live through Gail's experiences.

'Is it heartbreaking working with sick children?' her mother asked.

'I've only been there a couple of days, Mum, but I think I'm going to love it.'

'Are they all seriously ill?'

Gail laughed dismissively. 'Of course not. They're just the same as adults apart from recovering much quicker.'

'I suppose so. What are the people you work with like?'

Gail took a deep breath. 'They are all very friendly, including the consultant, who only started the job yesterday.'

'What's he like? Is he married?' her mother asked eagerly.

Gail didn't answer immediately, then she said quietly, 'You know him, Mum.'

'I do? You mean it's someone you've worked with before?'

She shook her head. 'It's Matt Roberts, Mum.'

Her mother gave a strangled shriek and grabbed her roughly by the upper arms, 'Matt? How could you, Gail?'

She slowly and deliberately removed her mother's clutching hands and propelled her through to an easy chair. She knelt down in front of her. 'I had no idea until I started there yesterday morning.'

'You can't stay there. You must leave. At once. Not go back—'

'Of course I can't leave just like that. What about the patients—and my career?' Gail took the seat opposite. The instant she had recognised Matt the day before she had dreaded this moment, and knew this was partly what had motivated her to come and talk to her mother that evening.

'But—' she glowered at her daughter, tears brimming behind her eyelids '—he's—he's—'

'A very good and caring consultant,' Gail finished for her quietly. 'I know how you feel, Mum. I felt the same way yesterday, but I'm not prepared to throw my whole career away for him. He's not worth it. And that's what I'd be doing if I walked out. You wouldn't want that either, would you?'

Her mother slowly shook her head. 'I—no. Oh, Gail, you poor child.'

Recognising her mother's anger was turning into compassion for the situation her daughter found herself in, she said briskly, 'It's only for six months. I'll live—at least I will if I get that cup of coffee and sandwich.'

Her mother bustled contritely back to the cooker and, relieved, Gail realised she no longer needed to unburden herself of her angst following the events of the evening. She *would* live and so, hopefully happily, would Mr Bertoli.

It was all just a matter of time. He needed time to come to terms with the death of his daughter, and this six months working with Matt would be over before *she* knew it. It wasn't as if he was going to be difficult to work with. It was clearly a happy department and she wouldn't do anything to mar that.

'Bacon sandwich OK?' her mother called.

It sounded wonderful. She might have missed out on a cooked meal again, but it was worth it. To have one of her mother's delicious bacon sarnies while at the same time feeling she had regained control of her life was a bonus.

For, since she had realised Matt was her new consultant, it had been as if her whole world was turned upside down and it hadn't been easy to decide which was the right course of action.

It had only taken a few moments' chat with her mother, away from the incestuous hospital environment, for her to see things clearly and to recognise how ridiculous it was to worry. She could handle the professional contact and, as they would never meet outside working hours, she had been foolish to think she couldn't cope with the situation.

'That smells wonderful,' she told her mother when she joined her in the kitchen. They perched up at the breakfast bar, and, as she wasn't eating, her mother started on the subject of Matt again.

'You must never forget he was responsible for your brother's death,'

'I won't. I can't, Mum. I miss George as much as you, but life does have to go on.' Her mother's irrational refusal to accept that she couldn't alter the situation by her hatred of Matt made Gail recognise how easy it would be to ruin her own life by behaving in a similar way.

Her mother, however, made it clear that she would never believe a good word about Matt and continued to harangue her daughter on the subject for nearly half an hour.

Eventually Gail managed to steer the conversation away in another direction.

'All right if I stay tonight, Mum? I don't have to be at the clinic until half eight tomorrow morning.'

'Lovely, dear. Your bed's always made up.'

Gail slept much better then she had the previous night and was up early for her journey back to the hospital.

Her mother had been up even earlier. 'I've made your breakfast. Bacon and eggs. Toast and coffee.'

Gail tried not to show her dismay. 'Thanks, Mum. Smells good.'

'The roads sound nasty. I just heard the traffic report on the radio. We had freezing rain last night.'

'I'll be careful.'

'You do that. And let me know the moment you arrive safely, won't you?'

Gail soon knew the radio had been right about the weather. As she made her way out to the car she could barely remain on her feet. Still, she reasoned, most of the roads into the hospital would have been gritted, and after a cheery wave of farewell she drove carefully out of the drive.

Driving was dicey on the side roads, but fine once she got onto the main road. Her mind turned to thoughts of Matt, and then to her mother's bitterness about him.

If he hadn't reappeared on the scene would her mother eventually have accepted the fact that it was doing her no good?

Gail doubted it. Her mother was determined to neither forget nor forgive and, though Gail would not forget, she had her life ahead of her and would do her utmost to make it a good one as she was sure George would have wanted.

With that resolution in mind, she indicated her intention to turn into the road which some miles further along passed the hospital.

It was then that it happened. A car coming in the opposite direction must have braked suddenly on an untreated patch of ice and he skidded across the road, first away from Gail towards a couple of parked cars, then, as he tried to wrench the wheel to avoid them, straight into the front off-side of her treasured Ka.

Gail saw the vehicle coming towards her and quickly released the brake to lessen the impact, but although doing so did limit the damage to the front of her car she was pushed into the car behind.

She groaned, switched off the engine, and resting her head on her hand, leaned on the steering wheel to watch the other driver approach.

'I say, I'm awfully sorry. Are you all right?'

She nodded. 'I think I am, but I can't say the same for my car.'

He grinned. 'My insurance will take care of that.'

The inevitable crowd had gathered round them and amongst the voices Gail could hear angry requests to get the three cars moved out of the way. She climbed out to inspect the damage and found her legs unwilling to support her for a moment.

When she could eventually move, she discovered the driver behind had used his mobile phone to call the police.

As there was no injury, they soon had the three cars moved to the side of the road and the traffic started to flow again, albeit with difficulty.

She asked the mobile owner if she could ring the hospital. 'I'm a doctor and they'll be wondering where I am.'

One of the policeman overheard and asked if she was on her way to an emergency, 'No. Only to start a clinic.'

He said he would ring and give them a message.

It took much longer than she would have believed possible to exchange paperwork and arrange for her car to be removed and she was relieved when one of the policemen eventually offered to drop her at the hospital gate.

Matt had been called in just before six to see one of his asthmatic patients who had been brought to the accident and emergency department by his worried mother.

To give him his due, the locum casualty officer had only asked for advice, but Matt had insisted he came in to see the boy for himself. The lad had already been responding to treatment by the time Matt had arrived, but he'd decided it hadn't been worth going home again through the rush hour and had breakfasted in the canteen.

He was first into the chest clinic and, finding no one else there, he carried the notes for the day's clinic down to his room. It seemed everybody was late. Due to the weather, no doubt.

When she eventually arrived, Betty lost no opportunity in informing him of the reason. 'There's been a three-car pile-up on the main road. Looks like a Ka was sandwiched between two silver Hondas. Funny that, the two bigger cars being the same make and the same colour.'

'Anybody hurt?' Not really interested, Matt asked the question automatically.

'There was quite a crowd on the side and the police were there, but I didn't see an ambulance. Mind, it could have been and gone.'

Matt nodded.

'Pam must be held up in the resulting jam as well. Lucky I left early, wasn't it?'

He agreed it was.

Betty went to answer the telephone's summons.

She came racing back, her face alight with news to impart. 'It was the police, Matt. Said Gail has been involved in an accident so would be late. Here, you don't think it was her Ka, do you?'

'They must have got it wrong. She lives in the flatlets.'

'I can check. I'll try her room.' She lifted Matt's receiver and dialled.

There was no answer.

'She must be on her way over. She'll probably be here in a minute.'

It was Pam who appeared next. 'What a journey! The traffic's horrendous. Must be the weather.'

'Of course, you come the opposite way so you wouldn't see it. There's an accident. Three cars—'

Matt grabbed Pam's arm. 'Do you happen to know what car Gail drives?'

'I do, as it happens. We were discussing cars yes—'

'What does she drive?' Matt demanded impatiently.

'A Ka.' Pam was puzzled by Matt's insistence.

He sank back onto his chair with a despairing groan. 'Not Gail, too. I don't believe it. I must be a jinx.' He leapt to his feet. 'I'm going to look for her.'

With a puzzled frown, Betty tried to detain him. 'I'll ring A and E. If she's been injured, we're the nearest hospital.'

Matt couldn't wait. He rushed out of the department and through to the front hall where he hesitated, trying to decide whether to take his car or walk.

As he reached the main door, Gail walked through it, obviously shaken, her face the colour of paper. He pulled her to him in a comforting hug, murmuring, 'Betty told us what happened.'

Sure they were being watched, Gail pulled herself abruptly away. He took her arm and led her towards the chest clinic.

'I'd like to go to my room, Matt.'

'Only if I come with you.'

'No—'

'Then you come where I can keep an eye on you.'

'I don't need—'

'I'll be the judge of that.'

Gail guessed it was delayed shock. She wanted nothing more than to have a good bawl. And she didn't want Matt Roberts there when she did it. She would be all right once she'd got it out of her system, but he was so determined she wasn't going anywhere without him that she allowed him to take her to the clinic building.

Pam rushed to take her other arm. 'Are you hurt, Gail? Can I do anything?'

She shook her head.

'Come and sit down. Coffee or tea?'

Gail didn't want anything but she said tea rather than argue.

Matt took her into the consulting room she'd been allo-

cated and pushed the door partly closed. 'I expect the patients will be arriving in a moment.'

Pam came in with a steaming mug of tea, Betty hovering
interestedly behind her.

Gail looked up and, with a supreme effort, smiled her
thanks and told them all, 'I'll be fine now.'

'I don't want you doing anything this morning. You can
sit in with me when you feel like it, but for the time being
just take it easy. Now what about your car? Do you want
me to organise its removal?'

'It's in hand. My insurance company is seeing to it.'

'Is it a write-off?'

She shrugged. 'I shouldn't think so but I can't say for
certain.'

'If there's anything I can do, or anywhere you want to
go while it's off the road, just let me know.'

Gail had to suppress a wry smile at his offer. The only
place she would be going in the next few days would be
home, and wouldn't her mother just love to see him turn
into the drive!

'That's better.' For a moment she thought he'd seen her
amusement, but he explained, 'You've got some colour
back in your cheeks. If you're sure you're OK, I'll go and
start the clinic with Pam now, but in the meantime I'll ask
Betty to keep an eye on you.'

Gail knew she should appreciate his concern and tried to
smile her thanks. Tried to make her smile genuine, but
knew by the resigned look on his face that she hadn't suc-
ceeded.

She finished her tea and walked across to the mirror over
the hand basin. 'Good heavens,' she muttered when she saw
her pallor and the way her hair was mussed by her repeatedly running her hands through it. No wonder he was so
concerned.

She found her bag and did her best to remedy the damage, then went in search of Betty to discover if there was anything she could do.

'Matt said not to let you see any patients this morning,' she responded gently, as if Gail were an invalid.

'I'm not surprised.' Gail laughed. 'I must have looked like a ghoul left over from Halloween. But I'm all right now, Betty. Really. It was just reaction.'

The receptionist grinned. 'Come into my office and we can chat between the patients arriving.'

Gail guessed Betty would want to know all the gruesome details so she could circulate them throughout the hospital, but she was totally thrown by her first direct question. 'Did you know Matt before you came here?'

Gail stared at her. She didn't want to lie, but neither did she want to confide in Betty. If only she hadn't protested her recovery she could take refuge in feeling faint. 'Why on earth did you ask that?' she said eventually, aware that her delay in answering had probably alerted Betty to her evasion.

Betty's eyes were gleaming. 'When Matt realised it was probably you in the accident, he said, "Not Gail, too. I must be a jinx." Or words to that effect. Pam and I wondered what he meant?'

'Perhaps he's had a previous colleague hurt in a car crash?' Gail was pleased by her quick thinking.

'Mmm, perhaps. But he was so dreadfully worried about what had happened to you and the girl on main reception said…' She realised she was perhaps going too far and said, 'Well, it was almost as if…'

When she hesitated, Gail prompted, 'As if what?'

To her relief more patients arrived at the desk to register and Gail seized the opportunity to escape.

'Is Matt free?' she asked Pam, who shook her head.

'Best not to interrupt. He shouldn't be long.'

Matt's patient emerged at that moment, and when Matt

saw her with Pam he beckoned her into the room. 'How're you feeling now?'

'Back to normal,' she fibbed. 'Could I see some of these for you?' She indicated the unwieldy stack of notes on his desk.

He frowned. 'We get quite a mixture on Wednesdays, but there are probably one or two you'll be able to handle. But only if you are absolutely sure you feel up to it,' he insisted.

'I do. I promise.'

Matt came in search of her as she was seeing the last teenage girl out of the door.

'No arguments today, Gail. Pam and I insist you come for a cooked lunch in the canteen.'

If Pam was there too she wouldn't argue. There was nothing she would like better. She was starving—in fact she had spent the morning rueing not having done justice to the eggs and bacon her mother had cooked. Her mother! Horror. She'd promised to ring and let her know she'd arrived. The accident had made it slip her mind completely.

'I will come, but first I have to make a quick phone call. I'll be with you in a moment.'

Matt didn't move but said softly, 'If it's your mother you are ringing, I told her you had a slight prang but that you are fine.'

Gail gazed at him in horror. '*You* told her! She spoke to *you*.'

'Well, not exactly spoke. More verbally abused, but at least I was able to set her mind at rest.'

Aware that she was staring at him open-mouthed, she closed it quickly and said, 'I'm sorry to subject you to that, Matt. It slipped my mind completely. But thanks anyway.'

'Any time,' he told her sombrely. 'It was nothing to what she called me last time we were in contact.'

'Why didn't Betty put the call through to me?'

'You had a patient with you, and when Betty told her

that she insisted on speaking to me. Luckily, I was between patients. Goodness knows what she said to Betty about me.'

And goodness knows what Betty is surmising from the call, thought Gail. She'll be sure now that there *is* something she's not been told.

Even while they had been speaking she realised that she really *was* sorry. Whatever he had done in the past, it was unfair of her mother to behave in that way to someone who was now a respected senior doctor. And her boss at that. A boss that she was enjoying working with and that she was finding increasingly difficult to think of as the villain her mother painted him.

For the first time since George's death, she began to question exactly what had happened on that skiing holiday. She hadn't been allowed to attend the brief inquest and—

Matt's voice broke in on her reverie. 'Are you going to sit there daydreaming or are you coming to the canteen with us? Pam refuses to wait a moment longer.'

She leapt to her feet. 'I'm coming.'

'By the way, I thought you'd like to know you've been spared one thing by your mother's call!'

'What's that?' Gail was immediately apprehensive.

He grinned boyishly. 'Betty was convinced you'd spent an illicit night of passion. She's quite disappointed to learn you were only with your mum!'

To hide the colour flaring in her cheeks, Gail strode ahead of him and muttered savagely, 'I'm starving. Are we going to eat or not?'

It was the first time she had sampled the canteen food and she was surprised by the appetising aromas that met them when Matt pushed open the door.

Even more surprised when she saw the quality of the meals. This certainly wouldn't be her last visit. She decided to try the roast lamb.

As they looked around for three spare seats, Pam saw a friend at one of the window tables and indicated an empty table for two in the back corner. 'If I join Meryl, you can sit there.'

Just what Gail hadn't wanted. To be alone with Matt when they weren't actually working. But he proved to be a humorous conversationalist on a wide range of topics that to her relief didn't include skiing *or* her family. And after his concern that morning it would have been churlish of her not to respond in a similar vein and she found herself actually enjoying his company.

'Do you want a dessert?'

She shook her head. 'That was very good, but enough, thanks.'

He nodded. 'I knew you'd enjoy it. Coffee?'

She half rose from her seat. 'Shall I get it?'

He pushed her gently down again. 'I offered.'

While he was collecting an ice cream for himself and the coffees, Gail watched from her corner. He was obviously very popular. Everyone exchanged a convivial word with him and it was clear more than one of the females invited him to sit with them, for each time he indicated he was sitting with Gail.

This made her an object of interest and in contrast to her earlier feelings she wished he would hurry back to join her. In fact, she felt a faint proprietary stab of pleasure that she was working with someone apparently so popular *and* that they were old acquaintances.

Which was contrary in the extreme when she remembered her resolve to carry out her work responsibilities but allow no other contact between them.

When he had finished his ice, she leaned forward. 'Matt?'

'Yes?'

'Can I ask you something?'

'You can ask, yes.'

'What happened to George?'

He regarded her enquiringly before saying, 'He was hit by an avalanche.'

'I know that. But exactly how did it happen? Where were you at the time?'

'I said you could ask me a question, Gail, but I didn't agree to answer it.'

'Why not?'

'Don't you think that, after this long time, things are better left as they are?'

She nodded. 'I suppose so, but—'

'Just leave it to rest, Gail. It'll only upset you and your mother again.'

'I don't see why.'

'It's not relevant. You and I are ships passing in the night. It all happened a long time ago and, although your mother might not believe it, the memory of that day upsets me as much, if not more so, than both of you. For that reason, I'd prefer it if we don't speak on the subject again.'

She was assailed by a sudden stab of guilt at causing him such obvious heartache and she knew she wouldn't mention it again. Her mother's outburst that morning had clearly upset him and, surprisingly, she now regretted turning the knife in the wound reopened by her mother.

The fact that after all these years of hatred towards him, nurtured by her mother, she could still feel so compassionate towards him made her only too aware that her physical attraction to him had never waned. In fact, the more she discovered about him and his work, the stronger it was becoming.

Banishing her thoughts as too dangerous to allow to flourish, she changed the subject and asked brightly, 'What's the programme for this afternoon?'

'One of our patients has been admitted to the high dependency unit. He's a lad of fifteen who we are soon transferring into the care of the adult CF unit at Papworth. His chest infection hasn't responded to oral antibiotics, so he's started on a course of intravenous treatment. Just as well. The lab have isolated Pseudomonas. I'd like to check on his progress.'

'All right if I tag along? I haven't a clue where to find any other departments in this rabbit warren.'

'Pleased to have you along, Gail. And if you behave yourself, I'll take you on a tour of some of the other facilities.'

She guessed his levity was a result of his relief at her not pressing for an answer to her earlier question and, although she wouldn't ask again, a query began to niggle at the back of her mind. Was there something he didn't want her to find out?

After another full day of cystic fibrosis patients on the Thursday, Gail was surprised to open the first set of notes for the Friday clinic list and discover it was yet another of their CF patients.

'I thought it was a TB clinic this morning.'

'It is really,' Matt agreed, 'but one of our cystic fibrosis patients turned out to have tuberculosis a couple of weeks ago, so we are now screening every one of our CF patients. I'm checking each one physically then doing Heaf tests.'

'Does that happen often?'

'Heaf tests?'

'No, patients with CF contracting TB.'

'This is the first time I've known it, but it does happen.'

'What about other patients with TB?'

'The numbers are growing. Especially amongst the immigrant population. Like young Ashok you saw with Vic on Monday. We seem to get an influx, then hardly any for a while.'

'Couldn't we have done the checks when the CF patients were in yesterday?' It seemed a bit hard to Gail for them to have to attend two days running.

'We've been gradually checking those who attend regularly, but today we're seeing some of those who wouldn't normally be coming in for some time. Ever done any Heaf testing for tuberculosis? Or Tine testing as it's now called?'

She shook her head. 'I'm afraid not.'

'I'll do the next one, then you can try the one after that, and if you're happy then I'll gladly hand the job over to you.'

Once she had mastered the technique, Gail enjoyed doing the skin tests for tuberculosis while he did the physical checks.

When they had finished she remembered she wanted to ask about the boy he had mentioned earlier.

'Matt? What's happening to Ashok? Vic mentioned we might have to admit him.'

'The nurses attached to his GP practice have agreed to supervise him taking his medication. They're a good lot there, so we shouldn't have any more problems, thank goodness.'

By the end of her fourth week there, Gail felt an accepted part of Lizzie's. Matt had done a good job that first Wednesday afternoon, not only orientating her to the building, but introducing her to so many people. She had friends, or acquaintances in every part of the hospital now, and she had even convinced Betty that his hug in the front hall after the accident had been nothing more than one of relief that he wouldn't be left as the only doctor on the chest firm!

She felt accepted and carefree that Friday morning and responded to Matt's casual greeting with a smile. 'Really feels like spring's on its way this morning.'

'I'm not so sure. If March comes in like a lamb you can be sure it'll go out like a lion. Winter hasn't finished with us yet.'

'Got out of the wrong side of the bed this morning, did you?' she chided with a grin.

Since Matt had made it clear he didn't want to talk about George's death, Gail had discovered not dwelling on the past had done wonders for her own peace of mind and their working relationship.

He had taught her such a lot, and she knew he was pleased with her interest in the subject and her increasing confidence. 'Any luck with a new registrar?' Informal visits had been arranged the day before for any interested candidates and Gail had met some of them, but not others who had come round when she'd been with patients.

He shrugged noncommittally. 'I suppose a couple of them were what we're looking for, but I'm not sure either were enamoured with working in London.'

'Why apply, then?'

'I suppose we'd do if they can't find anything else.'

'Great! Good to have such keen candidates!'

He grinned. 'The right person might still apply. Pity you're not further on in your career. We work well together.'

She was warmed by his words of praise, but, oh, so glad she hadn't enough experience to apply.

She might have been tempted, and, although she could sustain their working relationship within the boundaries she had set for herself for six months, the more she got to know him, she knew any longer would be a total impossibility.

CHAPTER FIVE

WHEN they broke for morning coffee, Matt asked, 'Any plans for the weekend?'

Dangerous ground! Gail had arranged to go home for the first time since she had broken the news to her mother that she was working with Matt.

'Just visiting friends.'

'Any sign of your car being returned?'

'Next week. Without fail. Or so they promised yesterday!'

'What about transport for the weekend?'

She grinned. 'Luckily most of my friends are in London. Actually I'm beginning to wonder why I bother with a car. Public transport is so much more relaxing.'

He laughed. 'I know what you mean. Finding a place to park can be the pits. Ah, well. Let's finish seeing this morning's little lot.'

Gail had only two more patients on her list. Both for check-ups and Heaf tests. Neither had problems that needed to be sorted, so, having arranged for them to have their tests read on the Monday, she settled to catch up on her paperwork.

Pam came in to see her as she finished. 'I wonder if I could use your room, Gail?'

'Certainly. Problem?'

'I've still got a few routine checks to do and Matt agreed to see one of his cystic fibrosis girls with a chest infection. Her GP rang in for advice and Matt suggested he take a look at her here. She just needs somewhere to rest where an eye can be kept on her until he's ready to see her.'

'Fine.' Gail started to clear her notes away.

Pam was back almost immediately with an obviously un-happy child swathed in blankets in a wheelchair. As Pam prepared to move her onto the examination couch, Gail walked across to help, and as she started to smile reassuringly she realised it was Emma, who'd shown her the fish on her second day in the department.

She took the little girl's hand. 'Hello, Emma. Remember me?'

As the little girl nodded, an obviously harassed Pam threw her a grateful look. 'I'll be back as soon as I can.'

Gail pulled a chair closer to the couch. 'What have you been up to?'

Still Emma didn't speak but shrugged one shoulder so slightly that Gail nearly missed it.

'Who brought you in?' she asked.

'That woman.'

'Mrs Grange?'

Another minuscule acknowledgement she was right.

'Where is she now?'

'Parking the car, I s'pose,' Emma murmured disinterest-edly.

Gail checked the obviously febrile child's pulse and noted it down, then asked, 'Could I have a listen to your chest?'

Emma pulled up her T-shirt. Gail warmed the stetho-scope in the palm of her hand and then listened carefully. She was still doing so when Matt came in. He closed the door and raised an eyebrow in query.

She removed the stethoscope and shrugged her shoul-ders, and told him, 'Her temperature and pulse are way up, though.'

He nodded. 'Mind if I have a listen, Emma?'

She barely seemed to register his presence and Matt gri-maced towards Gail, before examining the child's chest himself.

A tap on the door was followed by Pam ushering in Mrs Grange and rushing away again.

Matt crossed to his desk and pulled out chairs for them both, before contacting Jackie and asking her to see Emma.

'We need sputum samples,' he told Gail. 'Perhaps you'd like to go with Emma when Jackie's ready.'

Gail nodded and stayed beside Emma, but she could hear Mrs Grange's detailed replies when Matt asked when and how the illness started. Although she couldn't hear every word, Gail gathered there were problems at home; presumably Emma wasn't settling.

When Jackie appeared, Gail went with her.

'Have you been doing the breathing exercises I taught you?' Jackie asked before she started on the physiotherapy treatment.

Emma shrugged. 'Sometimes.'

'Not regularly?'

'Nah.' The girl pretended indifference.

'I thought you enjoyed doing the "huffing".'

'I did.'

'So why haven't you done them regularly?'

'*She* didn't let me.'

'Who?'

'That woman.' She clearly wasn't prepared to call Mrs Grange 'Ma' any longer.

'I can't believe that,' Gail told her.

'She wanted to do it herself. You told me I could do my own thing.'

'Yes, but only if you are doing it properly. It's for your own good to clear your chest completely.'

'Huh! Well, I was.'

While Jackie pummelled Emma's chest, Gail tried to impress on Emma the reason it was necessary. 'I'm sure Mrs Grange was only trying to help.'

Emma didn't respond and as Jackie finished percussion one side of the little girl's chest she said, 'You want to prevent your lungs becoming permanently scarred, don't you?'

Emma pretended not to hear and so Gail left the remainder of her lecture until a more suitable moment, but stayed throughout the treatment. Jackie handed her the samples Matt required and Gail labelled them and made sure they went immediately to the laboratory.

Emma clearly needed antibiotics to get rid of the bugs causing the infection, but they needed to know which would be the most effective treatment.

When Matt came to find them, he brought one of the clinic assistants whom he had asked to take Emma and Mrs Grange up to the respiratory unit.

When they'd left the clinic he told her, 'Until we get the laboratory results we'll start her on amoxicillin. She doesn't really need admission, but she is so miserable and Mrs Grange so unhappy that I think it would be better for the moment.'

Gail was surprised and asked, 'How long will you keep her?'

He sighed and shook his head. 'As short a time as possible. I'll have a word with social services this afternoon.'

'Social services?' Gail queried with a frown.

'I'm afraid so. Poor Emma. I guess this placement isn't going to last either.'

'Why on earth not?' Gail was appalled that the little girl's life was to be disrupted again. 'I only wish I had a home where I could take care of her.'

Matt nodded ruefully. 'I guess we don't really know her. I gathered from Mrs Grange that there are problems between Jeremy and Emma. According to her foster mum, she's resentful because he is healthy and she isn't, but I think there's probably more to it than that. However, it's not my problem. I'm just glad I'm not the social worker who has to sort it out.'

'Me too,' Gail breathed. 'I'd be far too soft.'

He smiled. 'I don't think so. You seem to have just the right touch with the sick children.'

His repeated compliments about her work were more than encouraging to Gail, so much so that she wished with all her heart that things could be different.

The thought of never seeing him again after her six-month stint at Lizzie's was becoming increasingly hard to bear. They seemed to have such a similar outlook on life, a mutual way of going about things that she guessed had been the spark for their attraction all those years ago.

'Come on. Lunch.' He grinned and raked his fingers through the curls flopping onto his forehead, trying to persuade them into place. 'Don't look so miserable. I'm sorry if I've depressed you with all this talk of the social ills of the world.'

She shook her head. 'It wasn't that, well, not directly.'

'What, then?'

'Just the general unfairness of life, I suppose.'

'No one is ever promised an easy time on this earth,' he told her quietly.

'My, we are becoming profound,' she teased. 'It must be our empty stomachs.'

She chose a ham salad and refused any potatoes with it.

'You're not dieting?'

'I sure am. Too many of those roast dinners are damaging my waistline.'

'I haven't noticed a problem,' he teased, eyeing her midriff approvingly.

'And a lack of exercise.'

'You should join a gym.' He pulled out a chair for her and nodded to the ward clerk sitting opposite.

Gail slid her plate onto the table and abandoned both their trays to a passing trolley before answering.

'I've never needed to before. My job has always provided enough exercise.'

He laughed. 'If you're suggesting I'm not giving you

enough to do, that can soon be remedied.' He winked at the clerk opposite, who blushed furiously.

'I'm certainly not complaining, but it's sedentary work, isn't it?'

'I belong to a place near the park. Within walking distance. I can take a prospective member along free. Come with me this evening.'

Recognising the danger in that situation, Gail was relieved to have a good excuse. 'My friends are expecting me for dinner.'

'More food,' he teased. 'How outrageous.'

'Why do you think I chose this salad?' she retorted.

'*Touché*, Dr Peters, *touché*.'

Much to her relief he didn't pursue the offer. Perhaps he had spoken before he'd thought about the implications and had had second thoughts.

They went up to see Emma during the afternoon and just the thought of not returning home with Mrs Grange that day appeared to have cheered her up.

'I see you're drinking lots,' Matt told her after checking her charts.

Emma murmured noncommittally.

'And did you eat your lunch?'

She wrinkled her nose in disgust. 'I didn't want it.'

Joy came over and joined them at the bedside. 'I let her off this time, but she's promised to drink lots of these special drinks this afternoon and she has chosen what she wants to eat this evening.'

Matt nodded and smiled at Emma. 'You'd better have a chat with Gail, here,' he teased. 'She must have been eating more than is good for her and needs to get some exercise, but I can't persuade her to come to the gym with me!'

Emma squealed delightedly at him turning the attention onto one of his colleagues, but, although Gail knew he had said it to try and encourage Emma to eat, she was still surprised that the subject was important enough to be uppermost in his mind when she hadn't given it another thought.

When he returned to the clinic to telephone Emma's social worker, he suggested Gail stay and chat to the little girl.

'There's not that much doing this afternoon, so you'll be better employed up here.' He left her with a grin and a wink and, aware he was remembering what she'd said earlier, Gail settled down to try and get to know Emma a little better.

It seemed he *couldn't* have regretted his impulse to issue the invitation, because ten days later he brought the subject of exercise up, again over lunch. 'I'm going to the gym this evening. How about it?'

'I'm on call.'

'I'll have my mobile phone.'

'I'd better stay around.'

'How often have you been called out since you've been here?'

She looked at him sheepishly. 'There's always a first time!'

'If it happens tonight, I promise I'll do your on-calls until our new reg arrives! If only to prove how confident I am of their infrequency!'

She laughed. 'You're on!'

'We'll go the moment we finish this evening.'

For the remainder of the afternoon she wondered if Matt had deliberately used his banter to trick her into accepting his invitation. Had he recognised her reluctance to socialise with him, and guessed the reason for it? Or had he thought she was playing hard to get?

The latter thought made her go hot and cold in turn and then she told herself she was being ridiculous. Attaching far too much importance to his invitation. You only had to look at his muscular frame to know that he believed in keeping fit and obviously thought it would be a good idea for her to do the same now she was doing a job that wasn't too frenetic.

The moment the afternoon clinics were cleared, *and,* to her relief, Betty had left for home, he told her, 'Towels are provided. All you'll need is cossie and leotard.'

'I don't have a leotard.'

'Not to worry. You'll probably only manage a swim to-night. They prefer you to have an assessment before you go on any of the machines.'

'I'll bring T-shirt and leggings, just in case,' she told him firmly.

'Not shorts?' He pretended disappointment.

She didn't answer.

He waited for her at the front entrance and she didn't miss the raised eyebrows of those around them when she joined him.

'Betty will know about this by the morning,' she told him as he reduced the length of his stride so that she could keep up with him.

He grinned. 'Somebody's probably on the phone to her already! Thank goodness after tomorrow lunch-time I'll be away from the department doing these interviews.'

'Thank goodness I'll be kept busy doing *your* work then,' she retorted spiritedly.

'You're not worried about coping alone, are you? I've cancelled the more problematic clinics and I'll be on the end of a phone line if something crops up you're not sure about.'

'I know I can contact you with the unexpected problems. But what about Emma? Are you going to discharge her?'

'Not immediately. I keep hoping her social worker will find her a new home.'

'Fat chance of that while they know she's reasonably happy here! And what if we need the bed? Medically she doesn't need to be with us, does she?'

'Depends how you define need,' he told her enigmatically.

'I suppose so—'

'So you'll cope?'

She nodded. 'With Pam's help, of course.'

'Of course,' he agreed solemnly and, placing an arm around her shoulder, gave her a playful squeeze.

Startled, she pulled away from his grasp, and to hide her disquiet at him insidiously chipping away at the barrier she needed to keep between them she muttered, 'Where is this gym? I thought you said it was nearby.'

'I said it was within walking distance. But I didn't say how long a walk.' He flashed her an innocent smile.

She glared at him with narrowed eyes. 'How long is it?'

'Long enough to start you getting fit,' he told her, 'especially if coupled with a swim.'

'In that case, I'd better put some effort into it,' she teased, and tried to speed ahead of him, but it took no effort on his part to keep up with her.

Cursing the length of his legs, because she knew she couldn't keep up the speed indefinitely, she was relieved when he told her, 'Turn right here. The gym's not far down on the left.'

He led the way through to a reception desk. 'Hi, Mel. This is Gail. I'm trying to persuade her to join us here. Is Ray about?'

'He's busy at the moment.'

'Any chance of him seeing Gail later?'

She shook her head and turned to Gail with a rueful smile. 'He's no free slots this evening, I'm afraid, but I'll show you round the equipment if you like and you're welcome to have a swim.'

Having noted with horror the energy some of the members were expending, Gail was relieved that she wasn't expected to make a fool of herself in front of Matt and told her, 'That would be fine.'

Matt nodded. 'I'll swim as well when you're through. It doesn't matter if I don't complete my full schedule tonight, Mel.'

During Mel's explanations of the different benefits of each piece of equipment, Gail tried to keep an eye on what Matt was doing. When Mel called to tell him she was through with the tour, Gail expected him to be too exhausted to swim, but after a quick shower he joined her in the pool looking fresher than she felt herself.

'What do you think?'

She grinned. 'If you can beat me to the other end of the pool, you've sold it to me.'

Without giving him a chance to answer, she dived under the water and pushed off with both feet, catching him unawares.

When she broke through the water at the other end, he was there waiting for her with a triumphant gleam in his eyes. She supposed she shouldn't have been surprised, but, having been the school speed-swimming champion for several years, she had thought she might just have been ahead of him.

She obviously hadn't taken into account her lack of recent practice. 'OK. You win. I'll join.'

When they were both showered and changed and Gail had made an appointment with Ray for her assessment, they set off back towards the hospital.

'Hungry?'

Gail immediately tensed. Eating with him in the canteen was fine. She could handle that. Eating elsewhere with him took on an entirely different connotation.

'So-so.'

'Italian or Indian? Or do you prefer something plainer?'

She inclined her head. 'I like either, but I already have my evening meal planned for tonight.' And there's not enough for two, she added under her breath.

'You could keep it until tomorrow, couldn't you?'

She shrugged. 'I could, but—'

'It would make a change to enjoy a meal together when we don't have to rush back to work.'

She sensed he was treading carefully, stopping short of actually issuing an invitation to socialise which he thought she might refuse.

Aware that it would have been a very different matter if there were no past hovering over them, she was sorely tempted to prove him wrong, but knew she would regret it in the future and said, 'I'd rather not, Matt, thanks.'

'I see.'

He was watching her and she couldn't avoid seeing he was hurt by her rebuff, so, not wanting to sour their working relationship, she told him quietly, 'I do enjoy working with you, Matt, and appreciate you inviting me to the gym.'

'But?'

'But as I said, I've catered for tonight,' she told him firmly, wanting to escape because his persistence was threatening her resolve.

Surely he must realise as well as she did that, although fate had thrown them together for this short time, for both their sakes any personal involvement was out of the question.

They were approaching the main door of the residential block before he spoke again. 'I'll see you in the morning, then.' That was all. Gail felt the breath leave her body in a great rush although she hadn't realised she'd been holding it. She had been expecting him to argue, to try and persuade her again, and perversely she was disappointed that he hadn't.

It was all she could do not to blurt out an invitation for him to join her for coffee, but after momentarily biting her tongue she wished him a very good night and let herself into the building.

His greeting when he arrived for the clinic next morning was friendly, but cool, and, though she had spent the night wondering if she had done the right thing, in the cold light of day she knew she had.

It was a busy morning as he tried to resolve all the problems that might beset Gail over the next few days and it meant he was late joining the short-listed candidates for lunch. He rushed off calling, 'Ring me if you need me, Gail.'

She didn't answer as he was already disappearing through the swing doors.

It was a surprisingly problem-free week and with Pam and Betty's help she coped with most things, so, although she spoke to him several times on the telephone, she didn't see much of him until he returned for the Friday clinic, which hadn't been cancelled.

When they broke for coffee, she asked if they'd found a new registrar.

'We did and I hope I'm not going to regret it,' he told her with a grin.

'Why should you?'

'Because I'm going to be totally outnumbered by females when she starts.'

'I see. What's her name?'

'Sara Wells. I think you'll get on well with her. She'll be starting a week on Monday.

'So soon?' Gail was surprised. 'Doesn't she have to give notice?'

'She's been working abroad. Could even have started this Monday but for various reasons we settled on the next one.'

'You must have known who it was going to be when you offered to do my on-calls until the new reg arrived!' she teased.

'I promise I had no idea.'

'She's happy to move to London, then?'

'She was one of the reluctant ones, but I think I persuaded her it would be worth it.'

I bet you did, Gail thought with what felt like a surprising stab of jealousy. Telling herself not to be so ridiculous, she asked, 'Will she be resident?'

He shook his head. 'She'd like to be, at least to start with, while she looks for her own place, but there are no free rooms at the moment. That's partly why we decided to give her a week to find something before she starts work.'

Gail nodded. 'Sounds a good idea.'

'Perhaps you could let me know if you hear of anything going. Living off site, I miss out on that kind of information.'

So, he would be in contact with her! Again Gail experienced what she could only put down as a niggling flash of jealousy. Whatever was the matter with her? 'I'll keep my eye on the notice-board in the entrance hall. I've seen the occasional advert there. What did Sara do abroad?'

'She worked with a children's charity in Rwanda.'

Gail was impressed. 'That can't have been easy.'

'I don't think it was. But you can ask her yourself in a couple of weeks. I'm sure you'll like her and once she's found her way about we'll be able to do so much more in the department. We're already way behind with some of our annual checks and I'm very conscious that you've been thrown in at the deep end.'

'Maybe, but you haven't left me to sink without trace— and I've quite enjoyed the challenge.'

'I've noticed that. Talking about challenges, how did your assessment go at the gym?'

'I put it off until next week.'

'Which day?'

'Er, I haven't settled on one yet. I said I'd let Ray know.'

'Chickening out already?'

Although she knew he was teasing, she defended herself hotly. 'I *have* been on my own in the department.'

'I know that,' he told her quietly, 'and I'm very pleased

with the way you've taken care of my clinics. But you need to take care of yourself as well.'

'I'll ring on Monday.'

'Why not do it now?'

She sighed. 'I'm not sure—'

He lifted the receiver and secured an outside line, then dialled a number he obviously knew by heart. 'I'm going Monday again, so we can go together if Ray can fit you in.'

Reluctantly she made the appointment for seven on Monday and the moment she replaced the receiver he told her, 'And when you do your shopping this weekend, you don't need to get anything in for Monday. We'll eat afterwards.'

He didn't give her any option this time, and she couldn't see a way of refusing without making their work situation impossible.

'Is that OK?' he prompted when she didn't answer.

'I'm on call,' she told him evasively.

'No problem. I can be contacted as before.'

'In that case, thanks.' She drained her coffee-cup and, checking her watch, said, 'I expect my next lad is here already.'

Matt smiled wryly as he watched her leave the room. What a mess. When he had realised it was Gail's car involved in the accident he had been nearly out of his mind with worry until he'd found out she wasn't injured. Something that could only mean that he was not only still attracted to Gail, but daily falling deeper in love with her.

And not just because of her looks and personality which had been the attraction when she had been just a teenager. Now it was a mature appreciation based on their shared interest in the patients and the way they worked together so harmoniously.

The more he got to know her, the more he realised how

happy they could have been together. If it hadn't been for the death of her brother.

An insurmountable problem, because, although he'd done his best to rescue George and his skiing companion, he blamed himself as much as Gail's mother blamed him. But for different reasons.

She believed he was a coward who'd run off and left his friend to die. Only he knew that he'd been too far behind to save their lives, but that he'd put his own life in danger to try.

But he still blamed himself, because he hadn't tried harder to stop George going on the foolhardy expedition, or, when he had failed, gone with him to continue his cautioning.

George's death had been such a waste because he would probably have made an excellent doctor. That knowledge had affected him more than Mrs Peters treating him like a leper.

So over the years he had thrown himself headlong into his work to try and forget and to try and make a difference in the world as George would have done. His ambition had left no time for serious relationships and, in any case, he felt that with George dead he didn't deserve any happiness.

Then Gail had miraculously appeared in the department and he'd recognised another reason for his reluctance to become involved. She lived on in his memory and he so wanted her to know the truth, but he couldn't tell her now, so long afterwards.

It would seem as if he was running down George to absolve himself and criticising her mother's stance against him into the bargain.

When they had first started working together and he'd realised what she meant to him, he had hoped to gradually build up a relationship with her that would withstand him telling her the truth.

But here she was, well into her six-month attachment and

she was still keeping him rigidly at arm's length. And for all his expertise at dealing with his young patients, he couldn't fathom a way of doing anything about Gail.

His thoughts were disturbed by his telephone ringing.

'Matt Roberts,' he barked into the receiver more brusquely than he had intended.

He groaned inwardly when he realised it was Gail. 'Er, when you have a moment, Matt, I'd appreciate a second opinion.'

'I'll be there immediately.' He replaced the receiver and made his way along to her consulting room.

She closed the door to the adjoining examination room.

'I have Anthony Cross and his mother in there. He's eleven months old.' She handed him the case notes. 'Vic saw him a couple of months ago. His GP referred him as a wheezy baby, but Vic found no sign of it when he saw him and said we'd look at him again today.'

'And?' Matt flicked through the notes. 'Not a lot to go on, is there? Can *you* hear a wheeze?'

She nodded. 'Quite pronounced. His mother says he's had a bit of a runny nose for two or three days, but she put it down to teething. He's not acutely distressed but he's certainly not a well baby and is off his food. Not too serious a problem as he's decidedly plump.'

'I'll take a look,' he told her.

Gail nursed the baby while Matt questioned his mother and then she helped him examine the child.

'Is he usually an active child?'

His mother nodded. 'You can say that again. I'm surprised he's not wriggling all over the place.'

When Matt had finished his examination he took Anthony from Gail and perched on the edge of the bed with him in his arms. He indicated Mrs Cross should sit down.

'What is it, Doctor? Do you know?' Anthony's mother

asked anxiously, then whispered fearfully, 'It isn't serious, is it?'

'I don't think so for one moment, but as you can see for yourself he is obviously unwell today, so I think we ought to keep an eye on him for a few days. Would you be able to stay with him if we take him into the ward?'

She nodded. 'What do you think's the matter?'

'I think your GP is probably right about the asthma. I just want to make absolutely certain there's nothing else. If you'd like to wait there for a few moments, I'll make the arrangements.'

He closed the examination room door behind him and frowned. 'Any ideas?' he asked Gail.

She shook her head. 'Don't you believe it's asthma?'

'I'm almost sure it is, but there's just a chance it could be bronchiolitis, in which case I'd rather he was where we can keep an eye on him for the weekend.'

'And start him on antibiotics?'

Matt shook his head. 'Not unless there's evidence of pneumonia developing. Any infection of the bronchioles is usually viral.'

'Sorry, it's something I haven't come across before.'

He smiled dismissively. 'I can lend you a book that'll tell you all about it, apart from a definitive way of deciding which is the correct diagnosis! We have to work that out for ourselves!'

He rang the respiratory unit and told Joy he was sending her a new patient, then, having made a few notes, asked Gail if she'd mind going with mother and baby to the unit.

When she agreed, he said, 'Tell Joy just to record heart and respiratory rate for the moment and ring me if she's worried. I'll be up to see him later.'

Gail did as he asked and returned to the unit thinking about the boy and Matt's open mind on the diagnosis. If she was

going to continue in this speciality she certainly had a lot
to learn, but she couldn't have a better tutor than Matt.

She sighed deeply as she made her way through to the
clinic. That was the trouble. She couldn't have found a
better working colleague, a better friend, even... She shook
her head angrily, before her conscious thoughts had a
chance to dwell on him ever being more than that.

Betty greeted her with a speculative smile. 'His lord and
master wants you to join him in his consulting room.'

Aware that the receptionist was still trying to discover if
there really was something more than a working relationship between them, she grinned. 'Thanks, Betty. I expect
he has another unusual diagnosis to fox with me with.'

She tapped gently at his door and entered the room with
as little disturbance as she could.

She smiled as the mother and father of the boy Matt was
talking to turned to look at her.

Matt looked up. 'This is my assistant, Dr Gail Peters.
You don't mind if she sits in on the consultation, do you?
It ensures continuity of treatment if I'm not here one day.'

The couple nodded, clearly eager to agree to anything if
it meant help for their son.

'I'd like to take a look at James' chest now,' Matt told
them. 'Gail will take you through and I'd like you to un-
dress his top half for me.'

When she returned to the consulting room, Matt indicated she should close the connecting door.

'How old is James?' she asked with a frown.

Matt gave her a knowing smile. 'He's older than he
looks—eleven.'

She raised a surprised eyebrow. 'They treat him almost
like a toddler, don't they?'

He nodded. '*And* he resents it—that's very clear.'

'He's asthmatic?'

Matt inclined his head approvingly. 'You're very ob-
servant.'

'If I'd missed those signs I'd be a pretty rotten doctor,' she said suspiciously. 'But why isn't he at the Monday asthma clinic?'

'Good question! His GP thought he should be admitted, as when he saw him this morning he didn't appear to be responding to his medication. He mentioned status asthmaticus!' At Gail's frown he continued, 'He's one of the old school.'

'But even if we still called it that, he's not that bad, is he?'

'Certainly not now. Come on, let's take a look at him.'

Matt listened to the boy's wheezing chest very carefully and then indicated Gail should do the same. As she did so, she thought the boy's breathing became more distressed and raised an eyebrow towards Matt.

He nodded and asked his mother to slip on the boy's shirt, but not to bother with the rest of his clothes. 'Nothing to worry about,' he told them reassuringly, 'but I think we'll keep an eye on him for a couple of days. Just to check that we've got him on the right medication. Would that be all right?'

The boy's mother accepted eagerly and Matt turned to James. 'What do you think?'

He gave a slight nod, but didn't speak and Gail was unsure if he didn't want to or if his wheezing was making it too difficult to do so.

'I'll make all the arrangements. Wait there for a moment.'

He closed the communicating door behind him and rang Joy again. 'Hi, Joy. Sorry about this, but I've got another admission for you. This time an eleven-year-old sent in by his GP. With the weekend approaching I think we're going to have to discharge Emma. Could you contact her foster mother? I'll speak to her if necessary.'

Then he said to Gail, 'James didn't have enough breath for a reading on the peak flow meter so I do think he's bordering on a moderate attack. Certainly not severe—at the moment, anyway. But I'm not really happy about him. Could you go up with him?'

She nodded.

He scribbled in the notes. 'I've asked Joy to start him on oxygen and continue with his nebulised drugs, but haven't prescribed oral steroids at the moment. We'll see how he goes first.'

'Sounds sensible.'

'Oh, and before you go, could you ask Betty to make an appointment for Emma for a week on Tuesday and take the card up to Joy?'

Gail did as he asked and when a porter arrived with a wheelchair she helped the boy into it and then accompanied the family up to the unit.

Once they had James settled comfortably and had carried out all Matt's instructions, she had a chat with Emma. 'I hear you're going home so I—'

'It's not my home. Ma Grange doesn't want me. I don't want to stay there.'

Gail tried to persuade Emma that Mrs Grange had only been trying to help her, but nothing she could say would change the little girl's mind. All she could do was tell her, 'You're coming to see us at the clinic on Tuesday. Will you tell me how you're getting on then? Joy will tell Mrs Grange what time you're to come.'

Emma nodded. 'Suppose so.'

When she returned to the office, Joy grinned at her. 'You're on call this weekend?'

Gail nodded ruefully. 'Afraid so.'

'You shouldn't have any problems. Monica's on duty both days.'

'Thank goodness for that! Although Matt has said to contact him if I'm at all worried.'

Joy looked at her thoughtfully. 'The rumours are true, then?'

Gail reacted with horror. 'What rumours?'

Joy was clearly taken aback. 'Well, that—that you and Matt have something going between you.'

'No. They are not true.' Gail enunciated the words slowly and carefully. 'Watch my lips, Joy. They are not true and they never will be. Please make that clear to anybody who thinks otherwise.'

Furiously she strode out of the ward. Betty might not be able to discover the truth, but that obviously hadn't stopped her making up her own version.

CHAPTER SIX

GAIL strove to control her anger as she returned to the department.

Sure that Pam was probably as bad as Betty, she wasn't sure how to handle the situation, but knew that losing her temper wasn't the answer.

The department was empty and Matt was talking to Pam at the reception desk. He looked up at her approach. 'I was just coming to join you. How is James?'

'About the same. He was somewhat cyanosed by the time we reached the unit. His lips had more than a tinge of blue and his oxygen saturation levels were right down but they soon improved when Pam started him on the oxygen.'

'What's his pulse doing?'

'Steadying by the time I left.'

'I think we'll probably have to prescribe the steroids, but I didn't want to do so unnecessarily. I've just finished the clinic. Let's have a bite to eat and take a look at him again afterwards. Joy will contact us if she has any worries in the meantime.'

As they walked to the canteen, Gail remarked, 'You're very lucky with your nursing staff here, aren't you? Some hospitals seem to have a problem recruiting the specialist paediatric nurses they need.'

'Vic was great to work for. They knew he appreciated what they do and wanted to do their best for him. I'm trying to ensure they feel the same about me.'

'I'm sure they will.' Her unsolicited compliment surprised Gail nearly as much as it obviously did Matt. She might think it, but she hadn't intended to voice it.

'Only time will tell.' He sniffed as they approached the canteen. 'My nose tells me it's Friday. Fish on the menu!'

After lunch they made their way up to the unit where they found James' condition unchanged. Matt looked at the chart monitoring his pulse and breathing rate and, after checking his blood results and the chest X-ray he'd ordered, said to Joy, 'I was considering trying a single dose of steroids, but I think as things are we'll start him on a course. Reducing daily depending on his response.' He wrote the prescription on the drug chart.

Joy went to administer the drug and Matt had another chat with James' mother. Gail listened quietly until he finished.

When the boy's mother returned to her son's bedside, he told Gail, 'I'll pop up and see him later in the afternoon and then decide how I think you should proceed over the weekend. Let's have a quick look at the others now. Joy tells me Anthony's settling well.'

Due to a couple of appointments being cancelled, the Friday afternoon clinic finished earlier than usual, so Matt and Gail were both able to visit the three in-patients again.

Matt spent a long time with James, and then moved to the office with his records. When Gail joined him, he told her, 'If James doesn't respond to the nebulised drugs I've prescribed, don't hesitate to start intravenous therapy. I'd suggest this for starters.'

She took the paper he'd handed her and was relieved to see he'd documented the drugs and dosages.

'Thanks for this.'

'You know how to contact me if you've any queries but if you're at all worried transfer him to HDU. That's what they're there for.'

She nodded. 'I should cope. I had a fair bit of experience of asthmatics when I was on the accident and emergency rotation.'

As they walked back down to the clinic Gail asked him, 'Did you speak to Mrs Grange about Emma?'

He shook his head. 'I've spoken to Emma's social worker, though, and she's promised to keep a close eye on her over the weekend and we'll take a look at her on Tuesday.' He led the way into his consulting room and perched on the corner of his desk.

'I do hope she can find a home where she's happy. I know she's truculent at times, but I can't help liking her—and feeling sorry for her. She's been dealt such a rotten hand in life.'

He raised his eyes to search her face and she saw a tenderness in them that made her catch her breath.

'You really care, don't you, Gail? I'm afraid, now that it's known she has a health problem, it's going to be even more difficult for them to find somewhere for her.'

She reluctantly dragged her gaze away. 'I know it's silly to let myself become involved, but we *did* start in the clinic together!'

'I'm afraid miracles are in short supply these days, but I'll tell you what,' he teased, 'I'll try and find you a magic wand over the weekend.'

'Now you're making fun of me,' she told him, her cheeks flaming.

He rested a hand gently on her arm. 'Believe me, Gail, looking after sick children isn't an easy option for any of us. We do our best, but often it isn't enough. I often wish I could wave a magic wand.'

She recognised that hidden beneath the surface of his banter was a serious undertone. She wasn't the only one who cared. He'd just learnt to coat it with a veneer that allowed him to cope and she knew it was time for her to do the same.

'Right,' she changed the subject briskly. 'Any other orders for the weekend?'

His face creased into a smile of approval. 'I think all

three of the in-patients should stay over the weekend and I'll review them on Monday.'

The third was a toddler admitted a couple of days before with croup but who was improving rapidly. Gail knew Matt had ordered other tests as this was her third admission within two months.

'What if we fill that last bed and there's another child requiring admission?'

'You'll have to speak to Ben Harvey's team. I've already mentioned the situation and they can usually find a bed on the medical ward if it's needed. You can also go to them if you have a problem and can't contact me for any reason.'

She nodded, aware she should have known he would have made contingency arrangements although, after he had offered to be available, she doubted he would allow himself to move out of the range of his mobile telephone. He was too conscientious.

She was kept moderately busy during Saturday. As well as the in-patients, she saw three asthmatic children brought to the accident and emergency department by their respective anxious parents, but after treatment they were able to go home.

She spent much of the time that was left thinking about Matt and, after Joy enlightening her about the rumours that were circulating, worrying about agreeing to go to the gym with him on Monday evening and then on to a meal. It was bad enough knowing that people were talking about her. She would move away at the end of her time at Lizzie's and soon be forgotten.

Matt, on the other hand, was in a permanent post and rumours could damage his reputation if they get out of hand. She spent much of Saturday night wrestling with how to tell him tactfully that she wouldn't be going out with him on Monday evening, but she fell asleep without coming to any decision.

Jane, the staff nurse on night duty, woke her at five on

Sunday morning. 'Sorry to spoil your beauty sleep, Gail, but James isn't too well. I think you ought to see him.'

Gail dressed quickly and raced to the ward. James couldn't speak and was leaning forward on pillows to make his breathing easier. 'Nebuliser not helped?'

'Not much.'

'We'll try an increased dosage before resorting to needles.'

She smiled reassuringly at James and explained what they were about to do.

To her relief, James' breathing gradually eased and he began to relax and doze.

'We'll try and measure his peak flow when he wakes, then I'll decide where to go from there.' She stayed on or near the unit for most of the morning and when Monica came on duty after lunch she felt happy to leave the now comfortable James in her care.

Gail didn't sleep well that night either, and over coffee on Monday morning she tried to tell Matt that she hadn't enough energy left to go for her assessment at the gym that evening.

He laughed dismissively. 'Nonsense. After a weekend cooped up in this place it'll do you good to get away for a few hours. You're just trying to chicken out again, aren't you?'

There was nothing she could do but admit defeat, so muttering huffily, 'If that's what you think, I'll go,' she returned to deal with the TB patients he'd allocated to her that morning.

Before they went to lunch, Matt suggested they took a look at the in-patients.

Gail watched as he examined, played with and chatted to each one of them in turn, and then spent time with each mother until he was satisfied they were happy with their child's progress. No wonder they had promoted him to consultant. Working alongside him was the best thing that had happened to her since she qualified and she wasn't looking forward to moving on.

'Anthony and Beth can go home today, but I think James should stay with us for a few days longer.'

She nodded. 'I'll see to all the paperwork and join you in the canteen.'

'I'll wait.' He wandered back into the unit and chatted with the staff as they served the lunches.

As they made their way down to the canteen, he told her, 'You did well with James over the weekend. I gather Monica was very impressed with your handling of him.'

'I felt much more confident when she was around.'

'Don't put yourself down, Gail, just because medicine wasn't your first choice.'

She turned to him, her eyes wide with surprise. 'I don't think—'

'What I'm trying to say, Gail, is that you're a very competent and caring doctor and should go far.'

She felt an unsettling quiver of excitement churn her stomach as she acknowledged his compliment with an aplomb she was far from feeling.

As she struggled to feed her turbulent stomach with even a mouthful of the salad she had chosen for her lunch, she knew he was watching her.

'You're not enjoying that, are you?' he said eventually as she pushed the green leaves around her plate for the umpteenth time. 'Why don't you get something else?'

'It's not that I don't like it,' she told him hurriedly. 'I'm just not hungry.'

She could read the doubt in his eyes and hastily swallowed a small mouthful.

'You need to keep your strength up for your assessment tonight,' he teased.

She seized on the excuse. 'That's why I don't want to eat too much. I exercise better on an empty stomach.'

'As long as you have enough strength to complete the afternoon clinic I won't complain!'

She grinned. 'No problem. I can cope with the asthmatics!'

He led the way back to the clinic laughing and her enjoyment of her afternoon's work was enhanced by the knowledge that he genuinely appreciated her work.

When they had seen the last patient and discussed one or two queries she raised, he told her, 'If we're eating later and I'm on call, I'll bring the car. I'll collect you six-thirtyish.'

'No, thanks.' They'd be sure to be seen and that would only add to the rumours. 'I'll make my own way to the gym.'

He frowned. 'Why?'

'Because I'd rather walk and get a breath of fresh air.'

'I thought you said you were tired?'

'That's different.'

'How?'

'I thought perhaps I ought to be on top of my form for the assessment.'

'So you'll tire yourself out walking?'

'No, I won't. The walk will get me going.'

His look told her he didn't believe a word she was saying, but he didn't argue. 'See you there, then.'

She was undecided what to wear, but settled on casual trousers, smart enough for dining if teamed with a lacy jumper and warm black jacket. That way she could wear her trainers to the gym and put on shoes with a small chunky heel for their meal together.

She was only about halfway through her walk to the gym when a car pulled up beside her. Matt leaned over to open the passenger door and looked at her outfit with obvious approval. 'Very nice. Are you sure I can't give you a lift?'

Now she was out of sight of the gossips, she was more

than happy to accept, so she climbed in saying, 'I think I would be grateful after all.'

He grinned triumphantly and, gritting her teeth, she muttered, 'All right. You were right.'

'I usually am,' he teased, then he must have noticed she wasn't exactly amused. He rested a hand on her knee and told her gently, 'You've been on call all weekend, taking on and coping admirably with more responsibility than you ought. What do you expect?'

'Sorry, Matt. I wasn't looking for compliments. Just sympathy,' she added with a grin. 'It would have been better if I'd cancelled this evening.'

'I'm glad you didn't,' he murmured quietly, making her heart flip over painfully. She stole a sideways glance at his face, but his expression told her nothing as he concentrated on the road ahead. He was wearing smart casual trousers and shirt and she guessed he probably had a jacket in the back.

He didn't speak again until he had parked the car. 'I hope you get on OK,' he told her as he hefted his sports bag out of the boot. 'I'll see you around and if you feel like a swim afterwards, I'll join you.'

The way she was feeling she was sure that was pretty unlikely, but thanked him and made her way into the changing room.

Ray was pleasant and very encouraging, even when she knew she wasn't performing at her best.

'We'll soon have you in tip-top form,' he eventually told her. 'You came with Matthew Roberts, didn't you? I expect he'll take you round the machines your first few times.'

Quickly she shook her head. 'I won't be necessarily coming with him every time. We're just working colleagues.'

'Oh, I see.' Ray looked almost disappointed. 'In that case Mel is always there to help you if you're unsure about any of the machines.'

When he saw she had finished Matt joined her. 'Swim or food?'

'Food! Please! I don't think I've enough energy tonight to even do one width of the pool. But I'll happily sit in the Jacuzzi while you work up your appetite.'

'I think we'll give the water a miss tonight.' The dark eyes that met hers were gently compassionate, making her heart lurch unexpectedly.

She inhaled deeply. 'I'd appreciate that. I'll meet you at Reception?'

His smile of agreement was warm and she took the memory of it through to the changing room. But as she stood under the blissfully powerful shower she desperately tried to wash away the feelings that were insidiously attacking her resolve to ignore his only too evident masculinity.

When she emerged from the changing room, however, his greeting undid all her efforts in the shower and she felt weak at the knees as he took her arm and led her to his car.

As she secured her seat belt, he asked, 'Where to?'

She shrugged. 'I don't mind as long as I eat.'

'I think you said you like Italian?' At her nod he continued, 'I think that's the best food hereabouts and I don't think we'll subject ourselves to a long drive this evening.'

She knew he was doing it for her sake and she murmured, 'If it's not what you'd prefer, I don't mind.'

'It's my favourite. So is this place.' He was already pulling into a small car park. 'I think you'll love it.'

He was right. There was a welcoming babble of chatter as she pushed open the door, and the tempting aromas that filled the atmosphere made her stomach rumble embarrassingly.

'Dr Roberts. Eet is so good to see you again,' a dapper, moustached waiter greeted him. 'And your lady friend? You are so welcome.' He grasped her hand and held onto it. 'Aperitif?'

To Gail's relief Matt shook his head. 'I think we'll order drinks while we look at the menu, thanks.'

They were led to a table in a secluded corner and, having taken her seat, Gail looked around her. The tables were cleverly arranged to give privacy to every diner, and the wall lighting diffused a subdued pink glow over the whole area.

When they'd ordered their drinks, she opened the menu and gasped at the choice of dishes. 'What do you recommend?' she asked, too conscious of Matt sitting opposite to concentrate on her decision.

'Everything.' He grinned. 'What would you like? Starter? Pasta? Pizza? Or—'

'No starter. Just a pasta dish.'

'How about the dish of the day?' He indicated a board behind her.

She settled on that with relief. 'Sounds good.'

'It will be. I'll join you.' He beckoned the waiter who was hovering after serving their drinks and gave their order.

'Garlic bread with it?' he queried.

Gail shook her head and if Matt had been about to agree to the side order, he quickly changed his mind.

'I don't mind garlic,' she murmured, 'so don't refuse it because of me. Anyway I expect there's garlic in the pasta sauce!'

He laughed. 'Even so, I wouldn't want to overwhelm you with fumes in the car.'

'It's a paradox really. Garlic's supposed to be good for your heart and yet the bread is usually dripping with butter.'

'Surely that's what's so nice about it,' he teased.

This was better. She could handle this conversation. 'But it would undo all your good work at the gym.'

'Why do you think I go? I like all the forbidden foods!'

Their meal arrived on the largest dished plates Gail had ever seen.

'Parmesan, madam?' the waiter enquired. Gail nodded and also agreed to a sprinkling of ground pepper.

When Matt had done the same, she bantered, 'After what you said I was waiting for you to demand salt!'

'That would be sacrilege!' He savoured his first mouthful of the food with exaggeration. 'Mmm. Delicious. Don't you agree?'

Her mouth too full to speak, Gail nodded enthusiastically and they settled to their food in a companionable silence.

When the plates were clear, she murmured, 'That was *bellísimo*!'

'I knew you'd enjoy it. Ice cream? Sorbet?' He checked the specials board. 'Or the good old English stand-by, apple tart?'

'Nothing. Just coffee for me, please.'

He nodded and ordered two. 'Now, I think we've exhausted the subject of food. What shall we talk about next?'

Aware that he had recognised her apprehension, Gail felt her cheeks colour under his amused gaze. 'Lizzie's?' she suggested.

'Work is taboo. How about what you do in your spare time? Or your holidays? Or the repairs to your car?'

'I think all of those would bore you stiff. I seem to have been working for exams and on call for so long that reading is about my only vice. Even on holiday. I look for somewhere I can flop for two weeks with a pile of books!'

'What kind of books do you prefer?'

She coloured. 'Nothing too heavy, except towards the end of my holidays. Then I read all those books one is supposed to have read.'

'Why, if you don't enjoy them?'

'But I wouldn't know if I didn't try them, would I?'

'True. Who's your favourite author?'

'I don't think I have one. What about you?'

'Thomas Hardy, I suppose. But only because I don't

seem to have time to catch up with the latest offerings. Do you go to the theatre much?'

'I used to as a medical student. Not so much recently. Daft, isn't it? As a student I had the time and not the money. Now I seem to have the money and not the time.'

'We'll have to see if we can't change that. I especially enjoy comedies and thrillers. Not so keen on musicals.'

'What kind of holiday do you prefer?' She quickly changed the subject, then realised she'd have been better off sticking with theatre outings. She said hastily, 'Apart from skiing, that is.'

He told her about his backpacking trips as a student, then over the large pot of coffee they discussed his interest in archeology and water sports, and his love of foreign food, which she shared.

He was so easy to talk to that Gail couldn't believe it when he checked his watch and said, 'I think we ought to go—it's after eleven.'

He settled the bill and drove her back to Lizzie's.

'Thank you for the meal, Matt,' she told him quickly as he pulled into the hospital grounds. 'I've really enjoyed the evening, but, boy, am I tired now.'

The moment the car came to a stop, she opened the door and leapt out. 'Thank you again, Matt. Don't bother to get out. I'll see you in the morning.' She closed the passenger door and sped off towards the front door of the residential block before he could either speak or move.

He watched her ruefully and sighed. She had gradually relaxed throughout the evening and he had been sure she was enjoying his company as much as he enjoyed hers. But that was clearly as far as she was prepared to go. What had he expected? That she would fall into his arms in gratitude for a simple meal? He had known all along *that* was the least likely thing to happen. So why had he invited her?

Because he was a fool and he couldn't help himself. It

was torture being with her every day in the clinic, but never on their own. He had nursed just a faint hope that somehow they could put the past behind them and build a relationship, but it seemed he was clearly going to have to accept that it was impossible.

He sighed as he locked up the car and made his way into his flat. It had been worth the try, and he would invite her out for more meals and take her to the theatre if she would go with him, but he must expect nothing in return. He would even help her all he could to further her career, but when she left at the end of her contract it would be kindest to her to sever all contact. Even though it would probably break his heart.

Gail climbed into bed, her head in a turmoil. She had thought it was going to be a difficult evening but she had enjoyed every moment of it.

But she hadn't bargained for falling in love. Because she knew now that was what had happened. And she sensed that he felt the same, but was determined to hold back. For her sake or his own? She wished she knew, because then she would know if it was even a remote possibility that they could overcome the trauma that dogged both their lives.

They'd worked together for nearly two months—two months in which they'd proved they laughed at the same things, liked the same things and worked together well. But the spectre of her brother was still too substantial, despite him never being mentioned these days.

Embarking on any kind of a relationship other than working together was a non-starter unless they could both come to terms with the past and accept it was just that— past—and that the future was…

Was what? She shrugged and turned over in bed. Without a registrar he'd needed her. From Monday he would have his new reg. Her contact with him would no doubt then be limited.

Perhaps this evening had been just a thank-you meal for all her help.

She couldn't wait to meet Sara. She supposed it was natural for the speciality to attract more women than men, but it would have been nice to have another man in the chest clinic. Matt *was* rather outnumbered.

She laughed at her foolhardy ruminating and tried to sleep. But she knew, however she tried to make light of it, the only sure way of resolving the impossible situation was to finish her time at Lizzie's and never see him again.

By the time Friday arrived, Gail felt she needed a break, not only from work, but from contact with Matt. She was relieved that she was spending the next two days with a group of her closest friends from medical school. Since they had qualified they had tried to meet up for a weekend two or three times a year, if possible in a different part of the country.

This time they were off to Stratford. She was relieved to have a good excuse not to visit her mother. Her continual questioning of Gail about Matt was beginning to get her down. She just couldn't accept that there was nothing Gail could do but work with him until August. It didn't make it any easier for her to cope with the situation and she looked forward to forgetting all about Lizzie's and her brother for the weekend.

They had a good time as usual and she returned to the hospital looking forward to the advent of the new registrar. Once she found her feet, Gail was sure it would make working with Matt a whole lot easier.

Sara Wells arrived at nine on Monday morning. Gail had already been up to the unit to discover James had been discharged over the weekend. She was on her way to her consulting room when she was hailed by a leggy brunette with a tan to die for.

The stethoscope round her neck left Gail in no doubt as to her identity.

'Sara?'

She was rewarded with a friendly smile. 'That's me. Is my old mate Matt here yet?'

Surprised by the registrar's familiarity, she stammered, 'I—er—I don't really know. I haven't seen him.'

The clinic doors swung open as she spoke and Matt rushed in. 'Sorry, Sara. The traffic was foul. I see you've met Gail?'

'Not properly. You're the SHO?'

'Sara Wells meet Gail Peters,' Matt introduced. 'Gail's been holding the fort with me since Vic left. She's coped well, but we've a lot of catching up to do on the annual checks of our CF patients.'

Matt turned to Gail. 'If you could carry on as usual to-day, Gail, Sara can sit in with me, at least until lunch-time.'

Warmed by his trust, Gail said, 'Fine,' and she didn't think any more of it when Matt didn't join her as usual at coffee time. He no doubt had a lot to explain to Sara about the clinic. However, when they went off to lunch before she had finished with her last patient she felt somewhat discarded.

Pam must have seen them go as she came in search of Gail later. 'I'm going down for lunch. Coming?'

On the way to the canteen she said jokingly to Pam, 'I guess I'm back to being just the junior doctor now we have a registrar.'

Pam laughed. 'Isn't that always the way? You work yourself into the ground to help people out of a hole and that's all the thanks you get.'

'I can't really say that about Matt, Pam. He did tell Sara how well I've coped. And in quite glowing terms too.'

Her friend grinned. 'I guess I've got a touch of the green

eyes where Sara's concerned. She's certainly an imposing vision.'

Remembering Pam's comments on her own first day, she said, 'Perhaps she'll be the one to snare his heart.'

Pam laughed heartily. 'According to Betty you've done that already.'

Gail shook her head. 'I told you in the beginning that was the last thing I would do, and I meant it.'

'Maybe, but you can't control the way Matt feels.'

Gail forced herself to laugh again. 'Well, even if he felt that way last week, I've been superseded by a newer model. Would you listen to me now? I told you I'd be as bad a gossip as the rest of you once I'd settled in!'

When she had paid for her meal, Matt looked up from the corner table and waved. Gail smiled in their direction, but joined Pam at an empty table on the other side of the room.

She had only been back in the clinic for a short time when he came in search of her. 'Sorry about not waiting at lunch-time, Gail. Sara was starving because she hadn't had any breakfast. I thought you would come and join us in the canteen.'

'That's all right. I didn't want to leave Pam on her own.'

He nodded his understanding. 'How did your clinic go this morning?'

'Slowly. That's why I was running late.'

'Any reason?'

'It was just a sequence of events. You know what it's like when everybody turns up for their appointment.'

'Perhaps you and Sara could work together this afternoon so that she can get to know some of the patients you'll be handing over.'

'OK.'

'I'm just going to introduce her to the in-patient unit. Coming?'

'I went up early this morning but there was nothing outstanding for me to do. Joy is just so efficient! So if you don't mind I'd rather sift through these notes, but if you want anything done, give me a ring.'

'I'll certainly do that,' he told her with a frown and she guessed he was wondering if she was sulking.

In reality she didn't want to be caught out by Sara in front of the afternoon asthmatics.

She didn't have to worry. She found the registrar friendly and easy to work with and she certainly related to the children well. And all the fathers seemed very impressed! And yet Gail felt a sense of unease about her. She couldn't have put it into words and all she could think was that she too was suffering from a subconscious touch of jealousy.

By mid-afternoon there was no one waiting to see them, so Gail searched out a cup of tea for them both. After discussing the children they'd seen, Gail asked the registrar about the conditions she'd worked with in Rwanda.

She had some fascinating tales to tell, but also many harrowing ones and Gail wondered aloud if she would ever be able to cope with the situation as Sara had obviously done.

'You just get on with it,' the registrar told her. 'Matt said much the same when he knew I was going out there.'

Gail did a double take. 'You knew Matt before?'

'Why, yes. Didn't he say? We were at the same medical school and have worked in the same hospital a couple of times.'

Trying to convince herself it was not altogether surprising considering the paediatric world was so small, she asked, 'Was—was that why you changed your mind about living in London?'

'I don't know that I've changed my mind about that! I'll tell you when I've found a permanent base. Sure, it was a bonus to be working with Matt again, but the real reason is that it's a darn good job *and* it will look impressive on my CV.'

One of the clinic assistants knocked on the door and told them their next appointment had arrived, so the conversation had to finish there, but that didn't prevent Gail mulling over what Sara had told her for the remainder of the afternoon.

She didn't see much of Matt, or Sara, for the next few days. Every time she needed to consult him about a patient, she found them deep in discussion about one patient or another, and left them to it the moment she had the information she needed.

She thought they might meet up in the gym, but either he didn't go that week or he had changed his time. Not that it was important and Gail was beginning to feel much fitter for her visits.

She was finishing her visit with a lazy swim on Thursday evening when someone dived into the pool and surfaced beside her.

'Hi!' Matt cleared the water from his face with his hands. 'How's it going?'

'Work? Or the gym?'

'Both.' He grinned.

'Work in the clinic has been much easier this week, so I've been able to spend more time with the children on the unit and that's definitely a bonus.'

'And the gym?'

'Haven't you noticed the difference?' she teased.

He stepped back in the water and his gaze slid over her with an appreciative glint in his eyes. 'A great improvement,' he told her.

Gail ignored his flattery and broached the subject that had been uppermost in her mind since Monday. 'I thought you would have persuaded Sara to join by now. Especially as you are *such* old friends.'

'Sara said that?' He shook his head. 'I've worked with her before, but I wouldn't exactly have called us "old friends".'

'I thought you might have mentioned she was at medical school with you and George.'

'We weren't in the same intake and I barely knew her in those days. I shouldn't think George did either. I knew a couple of the other interviewees as well. I promise I declared my knowledge to the remainder of the interviewing board!' He laughed uneasily.

Gail couldn't work out if he was deliberately playing down their previous acquaintanceship or if it really hadn't struck him as important. 'No problem, then.' She dived under the water and sped away from him.

When they surfaced together a few moments later, he said, 'As Sara's on call, shall we sample the Italian food again?'

'Not tonight, thanks, Matt. I'm already later than I intended and I have things I want to do this evening.'

'But we haven't had much of a chance to talk recently.'

Although longing to ask whose fault that was, she shook her head. 'Perhaps once Sara is more settled we could have lunch together occasionally.'

He shrugged and she sensed he was puzzled by her remark. 'You're always welcome to join us for lunch, Gail.'

'I seem to have had my hands full most lunch-times this week,' she told him with a hint of acidity in her voice. 'Anyway, now there are three of us it seems silly to leave the clinic without cover—it's better to stagger the breaks and then none of our meals will be disturbed with emergencies and incoming calls.'

He was about to protest, so she said firmly, 'Right. I'm off for my shower and then home. I'll see you tomorrow, Matt.'

'If you're in that much of a hurry I'll give you a lift back.'

'No need. I have my own car at last. Good as new, thank goodness.'

She scuttled away to the changing room and as she pushed open the door she was amused to see him staring after her and shaking his head.

CHAPTER SEVEN

IT WAS nearly twelve on Tuesday when a small voice hailed her, 'Hi, Gail. Where've you bin?' A subdued Emma was standing behind her.

Gail had remembered she had an appointment with Matt that morning and had been looking out for her. She was pleased to see how much better she looked healthwise, but she appeared unhappier than ever.

'I had some other patients to see. Have you seen Matt? Dr Roberts?'

Emma shook her head and wrinkled up her nose in the usual manner. 'I saw another doctor. She said I was fine. I haven't seen her before.'

'She only started with us last week. You've been doing your breathing exercises, then?'

'Most days. But she still said I was fine.' Emma's face nearly slipped into a triumphant grin.

'So have you been in to do your breathing tests?'

'Don't need to. She said I was fine,' she reiterated.

'Oh, yes, you do, Emma Langdon.' Pam came up behind her and half carried her into the room set aside for doing the lung function tests.

Amused, Gail went to watch, then checked the results with her previous ones. 'You have done well, Emma.'

'I know. I told you I was doing me exercises.'

'And eating properly.'

'I eat everything I'm given.'

Gail ignored the suggestion of a complaint that perhaps she wasn't being given what she'd like. 'All of it?'

She nodded solemnly. 'I'll show you.'

'You're staying with us for lunch, today?' Gail looked towards Pam for confirmation.

Pam nodded. 'We said she could.'

Gail guessed that was more for social reasons than medical and felt pleased for Emma.

Matt came in search of her. 'Coming down to lunch now, Gail?'

'I've promised I'll watch what Emma eats.'

'I see.' He winked knowingly. 'Right. You can come down with Sara later.'

As he was leaving the clinic Sara's last patient went to make his next appointment.

'Wait for me, Matt.'

Emma pointed. 'That's the doctor I saw.'

'That's Dr Wells. Sara.'

Gail thought Matt didn't seem particularly pleased that Sara was joining him, but she decided that was just wishful thinking, unless he was putting on a show of reluctance for Betty's benefit.

Gail didn't bother to take a lunch break that day. She didn't feel like eating any more than Emma obviously did. Which was not usual for her. She couldn't remember when she had last lost her appetite. But it would do her no harm. Coupled with the exercise she was getting at the gym, she would soon have a figure to rival Sara's and she felt so fit there was no possibility that she was sickening for anything.

By the time Mrs Grange came to collect a reluctant Emma, Gail saw it was almost time for the afternoon clinic, so she made herself a mug of coffee and took it to her room to peruse the notes of the children she would be seeing that afternoon.

But for once she found it difficult to concentrate. Although she missed seeing so much of Matt, Gail had to admit having Sara around was making life much easier. She had also taught her a lot in a short time, and her experience abroad had given her a refreshingly novel approach to many problems.

But Gail found it difficult to really take to her as a person. It wasn't anything she said, or even hinted, and she was always friendly, but Gail sensed she considered Matt her own property, although she had to admit she wasn't sure that Matt reciprocated.

Betty and Pam didn't help. They kept urging Gail not to let Sara take up where she obviously believed she had left off.

'You're just looking for trouble,' she told Betty with a laugh. 'Registrars always work closely with their consultants. They wouldn't be much use if they didn't. Matt hasn't had any time completely to himself since I started. Even if he wasn't on call he's told me he'd been around in case there was a problem.'

'I know, but—'

'Well, now he'll be able to get right away for a break. But first he needs to know that Sara knows all about the patients and his preferred treatment regimes.'

'You're too trusting,' Betty told her. 'She's after him. Make no mistake.'

'Well, why not? You and Pam have told me in no uncertain terms that he's available. So what's the problem?'

'He wants you,' Betty said bluntly. 'And you're right for him. We both think so.'

Gail sighed. 'And I've tried to make it clear to you that I don't, and never will, want to be involved with him.'

'Why? You would make him—'

'It doesn't matter why, Betty. I just won't.'

'But you're not committed elsewhere, are you?'

'No, but that doesn't mean I'm chasing Matt. Please try and accept—'

'There must be a reason for it. I'm sure you'd met Matt before you came here. Hadn't you?'

Once again Gail evaded answering. 'Betty, the medical

world is small enough, but the paediatric one is even smaller. I thought you'd have realised that by now. Now, have you the notes for afternoon clinic?'

Betty handed them to her and as Gail walked quickly away she had to consciously steady her steps so that the receptionist wouldn't recognise how deeply their exchange had affected her.

Because she knew in her heart of hearts that she was jealous of Sara and the fact that her presence limited Gail's contact with Matt. But Betty was the last person she wanted to know that.

'Looks a bit hectic, doesn't it?' Pam nodded towards the list in Gail's hand. 'We must have seen more in the three weeks since Sara joined us than we saw in all the weeks since Matt took over as consultant.'

Gail pretended to take offence. 'Are you saying that we were shirking?'

Pam laughed. 'No way. I just hadn't realised there were quite so many check-ups outstanding.'

'You seem to know every single one of them. By name as well.'

'I *have* been here for the past eight years. When you can say that, you'll know them all!'

'Not me,' Gail assured her. 'I'll be long forgotten here in eight years' time. In one year, in fact.'

'Where are you going at the end of your stint at Lizzie's?'

Gail shook her head. 'I haven't decided yet, but I'm spending my spare time combing the vacancy pages.'

'What do you fancy doing next?'

'The same, I think, but not in London. I think it would do me good to get right away for a while.'

'Because of Matt?' Pam queried tentatively.

'Because of my mother,' Gail muttered with a dark laugh.

'Did you always intend to work with children?'

Gail shook her head. 'I knew I wanted to specialise in chest medicine, but I also needed paediatric experience. When I saw this post advertised, I realised I could combine the two.'

'And you've enjoyed it?'

'Despite being thrown in at the deep end.' Gail laughed. 'Or perhaps because of it.'

'Vic made this into a really happy department and Matt won't change that. You could perhaps come back later as a registrar.'

'I could,' Gail murmured pensively, 'but I'm not sure retracing one's steps is always a good thing.'

She was relieved to see the first patients arriving and Pam said, 'Here we go.' She grinned at the clinic assistant who had just joined her. 'Let's see how this lot have grown.'

While waiting for her first patient, Gail watched Pam weigh and measure a decidedly underweight eight-year-old youngster, then raise her eyebrows in Gail's direction. 'Don't you enjoy your food, Angela?'

The little girl shook her head.

'She's become very picky,' her mother told them anxiously.

'Perhaps you could have a chat with the dietitian while Angela sees John for her breathing tests.'

Gail looked into the next room. It was the first time the respiratory technician had been in the clinic since she had started. 'Hi. I'm the SHO, Gail. I gather you've been away on a course. Was it useful?'

'Very—' he grinned '—but I've missed seeing all my little friends here.' He winked at Angela who responded with a toothy smile.

'You weren't here last time I came.'

He checked her notes. 'No. It's months since I saw you so I expect a big improvement.'

Gail smiled at her mother and said, 'I don't think Lisa has arrived yet, but have a look at the samples of supplements over there.' She pointed to a table set behind an information board. 'You might find something Angela hasn't tried there.'

The dietitian came rushing in at that moment. 'Sorry I'm late. Have I been needed yet?'

Gail smiled. 'Mrs Longs needs to have a word with you some time. She's looking at the supplements while Angela does her function tests.'

Lisa rushed over to the samples table and Gail went to her room to await her first patient.

She was still waiting when there was an unusual commotion at the entrance to the clinic.

Recalling the events of her second day there, Gail peered out apprehensively and her eyes widened in amazement at the figure dressed as a clown being mobbed by practically every child in the waiting room.

Matt was watching too. 'Who on earth is that?' Gail breathed.

'That's Joey. Of course, you haven't met him before. When the chaos dies down I'll introduce you.'

Gail frowned. 'But who is he?'

'He's the grandfather of one of our older asthmatic lads. He's a children's entertainer and when he came with Roger to the clinic one day, and saw how anxious many of the waiting children were, he thought he might be able to help them. And, as you see, they love him! And he's made the hospital visit fun for a lot of them.'

'He just comes now and again, does he?' Gail asked with a frown, wondering how that would help the majority of their patients.

'He usually comes several days a week, but he's just had a hip replacement. I hope they don't knock him over with their exuberant welcome.'

'Are you ready to see Angela Longs, Matt?' Pam interrupted them. 'She's just finished with John.'

'If you're not busy, why don't you sit in?' he asked Gail. 'Angela comes to see us often, don't you?' he asked the little girl who, with her mother, was just behind Pam.

Gail guessed he was telling her that the little girl was one of their more severely affected patients and, wondering where Sara was, she nodded. 'Can you tell Betty where I am?' she asked Pam. 'In case Robert Michaels arrives.'

'He's here, but no need to worry. Sara's with him,' Pam told her quietly.

Gail wondered if she was being manipulated by Betty and Pam as she made her way into Matt's consulting room. Robert was definitely on her list, so why…?

Telling herself she was becoming paranoid, she brushed aside her thoughts and concentrated on Matt's handling of the little girl.

He thumbed through her notes. 'Let's see what you've been up to.'

Gail saw him frown slightly at what he read but he turned to Angela with a winning smile. 'John says he was disappointed that you didn't give a bigger blow into his machine. I think you haven't been eating enough to build up those blowing muscles. What do you think?'

Angela thought about it, then told him, 'I didn't have enough breath.'

'I see. Do you have enough breath when you're at home?'

Angela thought more deeply about this question. 'When I huff I don't mist up the mirror any more.'

'Even after you've used your nebuliser?'

Angela nodded.

Matt smiled towards her mother. 'Are you using the mask we gave you to breathe through, or is your mum still helping you to clear everything out of your chest?'

Angela looked at her mother who encouraged her with a nod. 'I don't like the mask. Mum's been tipping me up instead.'

Gail realised the girl was shying away from taking control of her own treatment and relying on her mother to percuss her chest to encourage her lungs to clear.

Matt spoke to her mother. 'And is it working?'

She seemed doubtful, but told him, 'I do it as long as there's obviously something there.'

Matt clearly wasn't happy. 'Pop in the examination room and I'll have a listen to her chest.'

When Gail closed the door behind them, he said, 'She's not doing very well at all.'

'Her mother said she's not eating properly either. Lisa has already had a chat with Mum.'

'Mmm. If she doesn't start co-operating we may have to feed her by tube overnight. But I don't want to start that unless it's absolutely necessary. After we've had a look at Angela, I'll have a chat with Lisa and Jackie. They both need to spend a lot of time with her.

'In the meantime, perhaps you could organise a chest X-ray and blood tests and I'll get Jackie to send a sample to the lab and let me know if she thinks there's still infection there. In any case I think we'll probably change her antibiotics and see her on Friday. But I'll take a look at the X-ray first, then have a word with her mum.'

When Angela, with her mother, had been handed over to a clinic assistant to go for her X-ray, Matt murmured with feeling, 'Poor kid. She's really got it quite bad. Did you see her finger clubbing?'

Gail nodded. 'Was she late in being diagnosed?'

'No, and her poor mum has worked herself to a frazzle trying to do all we suggest. All we can do is give them as much support as we possibly can.'

When Matt had made detailed notes in her folder, he smiled at Gail and said, 'By the way, I hope you didn't mind me handing Robert over to Sara, but I feel you've missed out on seeing some of these more severe cases.'

'Mmm. I suppose I didn't realise until now just how ill some of these children are.'

'I'm sorry about that. Before Sara arrived I had to hand over the simpler cases to you just to survive, and then I wanted her to learn my method of working. Now it's your turn. I don't want you going away from Lizzie's and telling everybody you've learnt nothing here.'

Touched by his explanation, Gail assured him, 'I certainly won't be doing that, I can assure you. I feel I know a whole lot more than the day I started.'

'I'm sure you do. Your help has been invaluable. But you haven't got all that much time left with us, so both Sara and I owe it to you to teach you everything we know. Starting this afternoon you'll be sitting in on part of most of the clinics with one or other of us.'

Gail nodded cheerfully. 'Sounds good.' Then, wondering if Sara was as happy, she added, 'I don't mind pulling my weight, though.'

'I should jolly well hope so,' he told her with mock severity. 'And don't you fret, we'll still hand all the dogs-body jobs over to you.'

'Phew!' she joked. 'You had me worried for a moment! I still have to do my on-call tonight, then?'

'Too true. Sara and I are going to a research meeting.'

All the pleasure Gail had felt during the earlier exchange evaporated when he told her that. 'Something interesting?' she asked automatically.

'Breathing patterns in babies and young children.'

'Ah! Sounds fascinating.'

He laughed. 'It's more interesting than it sounds. Obviously babies can't blow into a spirometer or a peak flow meter, but we still need to know how well the lungs of those we suspect of having CF and other problems are working, and that's not easy if we don't have a baseline to work from.'

'I can understand that, but I imagined it had been done long ago.'

'It has, but these results we're being given tonight are supposed to be more accurate! We'll tell you all about it tomorrow.'

'I can't wait!' She made the feeble joke to cover an uneasy suspicion that him suddenly voicing his appreciation of all she had done was because he had a conscience about going to the talk with Sara.

But why? Why shouldn't he? Sara *was* his registrar after all and he had no guarantee that she herself was even going to continue in the speciality when she left Lizzie's. Unless. Unless…he felt he needed to convince her that he didn't consider himself as Sara's property.

Though why was beyond her. She'd made it clear enough that she wasn't looking for anything from him.

Her thoughts were suddenly so tangled that it was a relief when the children who were in for their regular check-ups started to feed through to them from the other departments thick and fast.

She smiled each time she went out to bring in the next child on Matt's list and saw the waiting children gathered round the clown who was seated amongst them.

The last on the list was Robin, who'd been an in-patient in Gail's early days at Lizzie's.

'He doesn't look much better, does he?' she murmured when the boy had left with his mother.

'I'm afraid that's as good as he's going to get,' Matt told her. 'When he's older, he'll probably be a candidate for a heart and lung transplant.'

Remembering Mr Bertoli's daughter, she murmured, 'What a prospect.'

Matt shrugged. 'Some of them do very well. Unfortunately we rarely get feedback about our specific patients, but the results *are* improving all the time.'

When they'd finally cleared the waiting room for another day, Matt introduced Gail and Sara to Joey, as the clown liked to be called.

'You've had quite a change-over of medical staff in my absence, Matt.' He laughed. 'But why all the female medics? Is the light attracting them, or hadn't you enough to choose from with all these nurses running round after you?'

'Can't have too many handmaidens, Joey, can you?' With amusement glittering in his eyes, Matt ducked the expected onslaught even as he finished the sentence.

Gail and Sara both fulfilled his expectation.

'Right, Matt Roberts,' Sara told him. 'That's the last time I help you out with a problem.'

'And I've made you your last cup of coffee.' Gail laughed. 'You can do it yourself from now on.'

'See what you've let me in for,' Matt said to Joey. Then seriously he added, 'It's good to have you back. The kids are so much better when you're around, but don't you overdo it. You need to look after yourself as well.'

Before he left, Matt made sure there were no problems with the in-patients. 'Joy's on duty, so you should be OK.'

Something she was hard put to believe when at half past six Roz, a three-year-old, was admitted from the accident and emergency department after chest X-rays had confirmed she was suffering from pneumonia.

Her mother said she had had a cold for the past few days but had been coughing all afternoon and seemed to be getting rapidly worse. She was certainly very hot and her breathing was shallow and rapid. Even as Gail started to examine her, she could see her breathing becoming increasingly distressed and her pulse-rate rising.

At Gail's nod, Joy started her on oxygen and attached a monitor to check the level in the little girl's blood. Blood and sputum samples had already been obtained, so Gail started her immediately on antibiotics.

'Is she drinking plenty?' she asked Roz's mother.

'She has been. She's very thirsty.'

'That's good. Keep offering her as many drinks as she'll take.'

To Joy she added, 'I'll be in the office. Let me know immediately if there is any change.'

Having written up the case notes, she rang the laboratory to see if there was any infection causing problems in the community. None was known, but Gail wasn't complacent. The little girl was not critically ill, but she wanted to be sure she was doing enough to prevent her getting that way. She decided to consult her colleagues in the high dependency unit.

She checked the girl's charts again, smiled at her mother and Joy and was washing her hands when she felt an arm rest lightly on her shoulder. 'What's the problem?'

She spun round at the sound of Matt's voice. 'Wh-what do you mean? What problem? And why aren't you at the lecture?'

He indicated they should adjourn to the office and asked again, 'What's worrying you?'

'A youngster with pneumonia. But how did you know?' She pushed the notes towards him. 'Did Joy contact you?' she asked suspiciously.

'Nobody contacted me,' he told her. 'It was just a gut feeling I had that you were worried.'

Too startled to speak, she remained silent while he thumbed through the notes. 'You've done everything I would have done,' he told her gently.

'I know, but…' she hesitated '…I was wondering about a broad spectrum antibiotic as well.'

'Is she getting worse?'

'Not since she started on the oxygen.'

He nodded. 'I'll take a quick look at her.'

When they returned from the child's bedside, he told her, 'Unless there's a definite deterioration, it's early days to start changing the treatment.'

'I knew that really,' she told him. 'I just wanted someone to confirm I was right.'

'That's what I came for,' he told her. 'I'll pop in again after the lecture and see how she's going on.'

'There's no need for that, Matt. I can always check with the HDU staff.'

'I know there's no need,' he told her, 'but I want to. See you later.'

Matt slid into the vacant seat beside Sara as the main speakers were introduced.

'Where've you been?' she whispered.

'Lizzie's,' he told her, and when he didn't elucidate further he saw her frown.

He wondered at that moment if it had been wise to agree to her appointment as his registrar.

She was by far the best of the bunch of applicants for the job, but he had never been sure if she carried a torch for him.

It was after he had told her that he was not interested in a relationship because there was someone else that she had decided to go abroad. But at the interview he had convinced himself that he had imagined she was ever interested in him as anything more than a colleague.

Now he wasn't so sure. Her demand for an explanation was too proprietorial, especially after her complaining at him changing the lists over that afternoon.

For goodness' sake, she was the registrar appointed to take some of the load off his shoulders. Next thing she'd be accusing him of pushing all his work onto her!

He grimaced to himself. He was allowing the situation with Gail to get to him. It wasn't Sara's fault that his SHO was still distancing herself from him.

He pushed his thoughts to the back of his mind and sat back to concentrate on the talk.

Over the food and drink at the end, Sara asked why he'd been back to Lizzie's.

'I left something behind.' He wasn't going to tell her about his hunch.

'It must have been important. I thought you really wanted to hear this lecture.'

'I *did* hear it. I only missed the preamble from the drug company.'

She must have heard the irritation in his voice as she didn't press the matter any further. 'What did you think of the results?'

'Very interesting as far as they go,' he told her. 'I was fascinated by their methods of carrying out the research.'

She nodded. 'I thought about going into research once, but certainly after my experiences in Rwanda I know I wouldn't want to lose contact with the children.'

'What do you think of the drug company providing us with all this—' he waved his hand over the buffet '—when they can't afford the exorbitant cost of the drugs they need out there?'

'It's not as simple as that, is it? Drug companies have to finance their research by selling drugs in the First World countries.'

He was relieved to have diverted the conversation and they chatted inconsequentially until one of the researchers joined them.

They left together and as they walked to their cars Sara said, 'I've just about got my place into some kind of order. Want to come back for a coffee?'

'Thanks for the invite, Sara, but another time, perhaps?'

'You're welcome any time, you know that, Matt.'

'See you in the morning, then.'

They climbed into their separate cars and he waited until

she had left the car park before turning his in the direction of Lizzie's.

Gail was in the ward office chatting to the night nurse and they both looked up as he entered. 'How was the talk?'

'Good. I've got the notes of it here. You can read them later if you like.'

'I'll go and check Roz's obs,' the nurse murmured and left them as he handed Gail a sheaf of papers.

She laughed. 'A little light bedtime reading, I see.'

'How's Roz? Any change?'

'Neither one way or the other.'

'That's good. I'll take a quick peep and then we can both get off for a good night's sleep. Hopefully,' he added, crossing his fingers.

Gail couldn't sleep, so she ploughed through all the information Matt had brought from the lecture.

She nearly overslept, but managed to get up to the unit and check that there was no change in Roz's condition before making her way into the clinic clutching the papers he had left with her.

She was relieved to see that the first patients hadn't arrived, but Sara had. She was leaning on the reception desk talking to Betty and frowned when she saw what Gail was carrying.

'How did you get those?' she asked.

'Matt left them for me to read.'

'Last night?'

Gail nodded. 'He came to check on the toddler with pneumonia I'd admitted earlier.'

'Why? He wasn't on call.'

'He saw her when he was in earlier and came back to check on her.'

'You should have called me if you had a problem rather than Matt. I know you got used to dealing with him directly when there was no registrar, but now I *am* your next in line.'

Gail frowned as she saw Betty raise a warning eyebrow and move into her office. 'I didn't call him.'

'So how did he know…?'

'I don't think he did—he was probably in the hospital for some other reason and heard about the admission.'

Sara looked at her through narrowed eyes and stalked off to her own consulting room.

Betty reappeared. '*Did* you call him?'

Aware that Sara hadn't believed her either, Gail glowered at Betty. 'Of course I didn't. I said so, didn't I?'

'Did you?'

'Come off it, Betty. You were obviously listening.' Gail snatched up the morning clinic list and studied it closely. 'Is Sara doing the Heaf testing this morning?'

'Some of them. Matt says he'll see the ones that were read on Monday.'

'Does he want me to see any of them?'

'No, Gail,' Matt answered from behind her. 'I'd like you to sit in with me again.'

'But—'

Her protest was cut short by him taking her arm and propelling her towards his room. 'But first I want to take a look at Roz. Coming?'

It wasn't until the afternoon tea break that Gail was alone with Sara again and she discovered that, although the registrar's temper had simmered down, she hadn't forgotten their exchange of the morning.

'I've been up to see the little girl you admitted last night.'

Gail nodded. Having gone up to the unit in her lunch-hour, she already knew, but didn't say so.

'She appears to be improving. Probably due to the additional antibiotics Matt prescribed this morning.'

'Good.'

'If she was ill enough for Matt to need to come back and

check on her, why didn't you start broad spectrum antibiotics last night?'

'Matt advised against it.'

Sara seemed surprised, but changed the subject, first
making sure they weren't overheard.

'I think I ought to warn you, in case you haven't already
realised, but Matt is pretty much a confirmed bachelor.'

Gail was angry now. 'So?'

'You've been working very closely with him. He's such
a charismatic character, it would be easy for you to get the
wrong idea.'

'Well, I can assure you I haven't. Whatever his persua-
sion, it makes no odds to me.' Gail started to move towards
the consulting-room door.

'I certainly didn't mean that!' Sara was aghast. 'I just
didn't want you or anyone else to be hurt.' She hesitated.
'It's just—well—just that I happen to have known him for
a long time and know that there was once someone in his
life who meant so much to him that her memory prevents
him forming another relationship.'

Gail stared at her with wide-eyed disbelief. Was she
speaking the truth? She didn't ever remember him having
a female friend in the old days, only George. So it must
have happened since George's death.

'What happened to her?'

'That I don't know. But I know that if he can't marry
her, he's made up his mind that he won't settle for anything
less.'

Biting her lip, Gail felt as if she'd been struck a cruel
blow. True, she had believed from the beginning that there
was no possibility of anything developing between them,
but that was because of George. Not because he was in
love with someone else.

Over the weeks she had begun to wonder if she had been
mistaken. They worked well together and she felt relaxed

in his company and had even begun to wonder if he could possibly feel the same.

Sara's words had demolished any hopes she might have had.

CHAPTER EIGHT

DESPITE having decided to avoid Matt's company out of working hours, Gail became aware that he seemed to have developed the knack of knowing when she was at the gym and joining her whenever he could.

And when she refused his repeated invitations to join him for a meal, the expression of disappointment on his face was difficult to ignore.

At times, in the clinic, she sensed him watching her with an expression of profound sadness, and, although she wished with all her heart that he could find happiness, she knew that, as a reminder of his past, she was the last person to help.

The sooner she got right away, the better, and perhaps he would be able to forget his lost love, whoever she was, and start afresh.

She hoped so, desperately, because she knew now that his happiness meant more to her than her own. She had taken the first two weeks in May off as annual leave, and he had seemed so much happier on her return that she knew, without doubt, that it was her presence that was the problem.

She herself had never enjoyed a holiday less. She had deliberately persuaded her friends to join her at one of the parks springing up throughout the country with enough leisure pursuits to keep them busy every moment of the day. But however much she had thrown herself into the physical activity, it hadn't occupied her mind. Her thoughts had been at Lizzie's most of the time, and especially with Matt.

It was almost a relief to be back, especially that first

afternoon when she knew so many of the asthmatic patients who came in to see her.

Wayne Smith, who had been one of the first patients she had seen on her first day, was as crafty as ever. His asthma was well controlled, but as usual he told her he was taking the whole afternoon off school for his visit.

'I don't like you missing so much school, Wayne,' she told him, 'so I'm going to write to your GP and he'll look after you from now on. There's really no need for you to keep coming here.'

'Aw, miss, that's not fair. What if I get another bad attack?'

She smiled. 'If your mum has any worries at all about you, she only has to contact us and we'll see you again. OK?'

'S'pose so,' he told her cheerfully. 'Bye, miss. See you some time.'

That evening she slipped away to the gym the moment she finished work. Now she had got herself back to optimum fitness, she intended to stay that way. She was swimming lengths when she saw Matt coming out of the changing room and decided it would be fun to challenge him to a race as she had on her first night there. She was sure this time she *would* beat him.

She was swimming towards him when she saw Sara dive into the pool. She felt a surge of dismay and tried to escape without being seen. However, when she emerged from the changing room Matt was there waiting.

'I thought as we were both here we could eat together tonight.'

'No, thanks. And you obviously won't be alone.'

'Gail,' Matt began, sounding upset, 'I—'

'Goodnight, Matt,' she told him firmly. 'I'll see you in the morning.'

* * *

Over the Italian meal, his thoughts were with Gail and the meal they had enjoyed there. He had been so looking forward to seeing her that evening. She was looking so fit after her holiday that he guessed she would be visiting the gym on a regular basis. A chat with Betty had confirmed his suspicions! Somehow Betty nearly always knew!

He wished now he'd taken Sara somewhere else to eat. He felt her hand cover his and quickly pulled it away.

'What's the matter, Matt? You don't seem yourself at all.'

'I suppose I'm worrying about Gail.'

'Why?' Sara was clearly puzzled.

'She wanted to be a lawyer, you know.'

Sara looked at him suspiciously. 'She did? So what is she doing here?'

'Making a good job of her second-choice career.'

'But why didn't she go after what she wanted?'

'Because her brother died in an accident. He was a medical student and, as a widow, their mother lives her life through her children. I guess Gail read medicine purely to please her.'

'She seems happy enough in her work.'

'I think she is. At least was, until she had to work with me.'

'I can't see why that should be a problem?' The truth must have hit Sara with a punch, changing her nonchalant expression to one of horror. 'Oh, no! Was—was it her brother—was he the guy you tried to save in that skiing accident?'

'I'm afraid so.'

Sara looked at him aghast.

'Why on earth didn't you warn me?'

He shrugged. 'I didn't see any need.'

'I could easily have said something to upset her.'

'I doubt that. You didn't know George all that well, did you?'

'Pity it wasn't well enough to remember that his surname was Peters! The penny might have dropped then.'

'Gail and I have agreed it was all in the past and we don't talk about it. She's only here for six months. She's a good doctor and I hope I'll be able to help her career forward, but that'll be the end of it. For both her and her mother's sake, if they never see me again, it'll be too soon.'

Sara nodded thoughtfully. 'I see now why you feel you have to help her more than you would normally do.'

He frowned. 'What do you mean?'

Sara realised she had perhaps said too much. 'Well—like you said, she'll be moving on soon.'

'So? I'm not sure just what you are suggesting, Sara.' His voice was cold as he wondered if she was jealous of the time he was spending with Gail at work. Was that why she had decided to join the gym that very evening?

Gail sensed the change in the atmosphere the moment she arrived at work on Tuesday morning. She could only presume Sara saw her as a threat, but why, she wasn't sure. Hadn't she left the way clear for the registrar the previous evening?

Throughout the morning clinic Gail watched them both and came to the conclusion that Sara was very much keener than Matt, but, not wanting to be held responsible for his lack of interest, she tried to minimise her contact with him even further.

She avoided joining them for lunch, instead buying herself a pack of sandwiches from Mrs Lewis at Dunwoody and finding a quiet spot in the grounds to eat them.

After lunch she went up to check on the in-patients. Even the elements seemed to be against her. The sun had decided it was summer, chasing away the earlier spate of colds and flu, so there was only a couple of children in the unit. These were Angela, in for a course of intravenous antibiotics and intensive physiotherapy, and Emily, who had been brought to Casualty by her over-anxious parents following a mild exacerbation of her asthma. But both were on the mend and she could not find anything that needed doing.

She returned to the clinic, to find Matt chatting with Betty. 'I was just saying how quickly your time with us is flying by,' Betty told her.

Gail nodded. 'Have you found a replacement?' she asked Matt.

He shrugged. 'I haven't looked. I wasn't sure what you would be doing.'

'I'm looking for a similar post. Somewhere larger, preferably. I need as much experience as I can get.'

'Are you thinking of staying in London?' Betty asked.

'No. It's time I spread my wings. In fact,' she told them as Sara joined them, 'I rang up earlier about a job going in Lancashire. It sounds good. A very busy unit and they seem more than interested in the experience I've gained here. You've both taught me a lot, but if I'm going to remain in the speciality I think this is the job for me.'

'Is it a teaching post?' Matt asked tersely.

'I gather so. I'll try and speak to the present incumbent to check.'

'It would be better for your career to remain in London,' Matt said grimly.

Gail met his eyes and was surprised by the anxiety she saw there. 'I don't see why—'

'If I can do anything at all to help,' Sara broke in, 'let me know, won't you?'

Suspicious that Sara would be only too happy to speed Gail on her way out of Matt's orbit, she murmured, 'I will, don't worry.'

Matt was still holding her eyes with his and Gail felt uncomfortable with Betty and Sara watching. She tore her gaze away. 'Pam's probably tearing her hair out because we're all missing.'

She strode through the department nodding to the patients she was coming to know as well as Vic had on her first day. She settled at her desk and pulled towards her the set of notes that Pam had left there for her.

Matt followed her into her consulting room and closed the door behind him.

'I need to talk to you, Gail.'

'But—but the patients are waiting.'

He spread his hands. 'OK, not now, but before you accept this job.'

Gail frowned.

'I'll collect you at seven this evening.' He strode from the room leaving her with no opportunity to refuse.

During every lull that afternoon, Gail's thoughts centred on the reason for Matt's invitation. By three o'clock she was back to wondering again just what had happened on the ski slope all those years ago and why he had always refused to talk to her about it.

Did her mother really know the whole truth, or was it all made up? Because nothing Matt had done since she'd been working with him could convince her that he would be so uncaring as to walk away from his friend and leave him to die. And yet that was what her mother had always insisted happened.

Perhaps she could get him to talk about it that evening. If not, she had nothing planned for the coming weekend, so she would go home and quiz her mother, who no doubt would be itching to hear all about her holiday.

The decision made, she pushed all thoughts of Matt to one side and concentrated on the patients for the rest of the afternoon.

She didn't know what to wear that evening, but eventually settled on a plain dress that she could dress up or down with the sea-green silk scarf that she slipped under the collar of her jacket.

He took her to the same place and again they ordered

the dish of the day. The little Italian seemed surprised to see her and Gail realised why when Matt told her, 'Sara and I ate here last night. I'm sorry you couldn't join us.'

She nodded numbly. 'I think for both our sakes the less we see of one another out of hours, the better.'

'That's why you refuse all my invitations, isn't it?'

'Of course.'

He sighed deeply. 'Gail, since we've been working together, I've realised there's no one's company I'd rather have,' he told her quietly.

Remembering what Sara had told her, she murmured, 'Maybe, but…' Her voice trailed off under his intense scrutiny, and she found it difficult to tear her gaze away.

'It's true, Gail, but I don't want you to think I underestimate the angst I've been causing you.'

She lifted her head sharply. 'You don't—'

He seemed not to hear as he continued, 'I appreciate what an impossible situation this has been for you. But I have to stop you going up to Lancashire to work and ruining your career prospects in the process. Gail, I want you to know—'

'But I won't be ruining my prospects. The hospital has a good reputation.'

'Gail, believe me, I know what I'm talking about and I do want you to know that I'm going to stop pestering you with invitations.'

Although she thought it was what she wanted, his words twisted her heart muscles painfully, for a moment making it impossible for her to speak.

'I asked you to join me for this meal tonight because I wanted to make that absolutely clear.' He leaned across the table and took both her hands in his and said, 'I'll never forget you, Gail, and if there's ever anything at all I can do to help your career, now or in the future, you only have to ask.'

Although she wouldn't be leaving the hospital for a couple of months, she felt he was, in effect, saying goodbye to her.

It hurt, but she tried to tell herself it was probably all for the best, although it did make it impossible for her to ask him anything about the accident.

Once he'd said what he'd come to say, his mood changed and he became good company for the remainder of the evening, but she sensed things would never be the same again between them.

However, once in bed, she thought back to all he had said and the longer she thought about it, the more she decided she had completely missed the point.

It wasn't that he didn't really believe the northern hospital wasn't good enough, it was that he didn't want her to feel hounded into going there, or anywhere else, just to get away from him. In effect, she became sure he was trying to tell her that he cared as much about her as she did about him, but was going to butt out of her life so that she could be happy.

Why, oh, why hadn't he said so straight, she asked herself in despair, instead of going all round Regent's Park to do it? Then she could have told him how she really felt and perhaps, just perhaps, they could have worked something out.

The moment she saw him enter his room the next morning she followed him in. 'Matt. About last night.'

'I meant what I said.'

'I know, Matt, and that's what—'

'Leave it, Gail. I just wanted you to know you don't have to ruin a promising career because of what happened all those years ago. Now, I don't want to talk about it any more. Let's get this O and S clinic under way.'

He was true to his word and left her so severely alone that when the morning clinic had finished Pam asked, 'Have you two had a falling out?'

Gail grimaced wryly. 'It's not so much a falling-out as

a misunderstanding. I didn't understand what he was trying to tell me last night until I got home to bed and thought about it. Now he won't talk about it. Talk about stubborn! Mules don't come into it.'

Sara followed her back to her consulting room. 'I couldn't help overhearing what you were saying to Pam. Don't you think you're being a bit hard on him?'

Gail glared at her and was about to tell her to mind her own business when she had second thoughts. 'Maybe. This situation isn't easy for either of us.'

Sara clearly hesitated before asking, 'Were you talking about your brother?'

'In a way. Except that he won't ever discuss what really happened.'

'I'm not surprised. He was devastated at the time. We thought for a long time that he would give up medicine, but luckily it worked the other way around. He threw himself into his work and studied and worked hard to become something your brother would be proud of. It's a pity he couldn't find happiness with the girl he loved—I've tried to tell him that all work and no play isn't good for him but...' She shrugged.

'Sara,' Gail began nervously, 'I don't suppose *you* know exactly what did happen that day?'

'I heard rumours, but I wasn't exactly close to either of them. But it was well known that George was always head-strong. So it was all the more tragic that Matt blamed himself.'

'If only he'd tried to help after it happened, instead of walking away. Everybody knows those first few moments are vital.'

Sara frowned. 'But I didn't think he was there during those first few minutes. Was he?'

'He must have been. He summoned the emergency teams but he did nothing himself but save his skin.' She could hear herself repeating her mother's words and groaned inwardly. Somehow she had to discover the truth.

'It seems to me,' Sara began carefully, 'that you are recounting a totally different version of events to the one I remember, but I suppose that's not altogether surprising. Although I was horrified at the death of one of our colleagues, I didn't consciously listen to all the details.'

'I guess not.'

'You haven't *ever* talked to Matt about it?'

Gail shook her head. 'As I said, he won't discuss it. Says it's all in the past and best left there.'

Pam rushed in at that moment. 'Can one of you come quickly? It's Joey with his grandson.' They both raced through to the waiting room that had been empty a moment before. The boy was seated on one of the upright chairs leaning forward as he tried desperately to gasp some air.

'Oxygen, quickly and a nebuliser,' Sara ordered. 'And have the crash trolley handy. And find Matt if you can.'

'Let's get Roger into Matt's examination room,' she said quietly to Gail.

They carried him through and seated him on the couch with every pillow they could find in the department behind him and a couple to lean forward on.

'How old is he?' she asked his grandfather.

'Fourteen,' he told them in shaky voice.

As she worked out the drug dosages for the nebuliser, Matt raced in and took control. 'Get Betty to find Joey some tea,' he asked Pam.

She took the hint and led Joey from the room.

As Sara primed the nebuliser, Matt tried to get Roger to use the peak flow meter but he didn't have sufficient breath to register.

'Borrow the low-reading meter from the unit,' he urged Gail, 'and ask Betty to organise a portable X-ray machine.'

Gail asked Betty and then raced to the respiratory unit and back with the peak flow meter.

Matt thrust a chart at her. 'Keep a record.' He detailed the drugs given so far.

He tried again to get a peak flow reading, but it was impossible.

'Keep a record of his blood gases as well,' he told Gail.

'They're rising,' Sara told them. 'He needs to go to ITU.'

'I'll check the beds.'

Gail made all the arrangements and within minutes Roger was on his way to the intensive therapy unit with Matt and Sara in attendance.

'Look after Joey,' Matt called to Gail, 'and divert the radiographer.'

Betty was trying ineffectually to console Joey when Gail offered to take him up to ITU. She gave Gail a relieved smile and relinquished her post.

It was mid-afternoon when Matt returned to the clinic. Gail was struggling to deal with the afternoon list of CF patients whose Heaf test readings hadn't been conclusive on Monday.

'How is Roger?' she asked when she had a moment.

'Not responding markedly. Sara's staying up there to liaise with the ITU team. They may have to ventilate.'

'Poor lad. Do we know what triggered the attack?'

'Not really. He has a games period at school on Wednesday mornings and goes to his grandfather for lunch, but when he arrived today he could hardly speak and as Joey drove him here he just got worse. Thank goodness Joey did bring him straight here or it might have been too late. Now, how are you coping?'

'With difficulty,' she told him. 'There's a couple I'd like you to see.'

'What about the rest?'

'All done.'

'You've done well,' he told her.

'Before I forget, Matt, can I ask you about that baby with what Vic thought was floppy larynx? I saw he was here this morning and it's the first chance I've had to ask how he's doing?'

'He's fine. Vic's diagnosis was spot on.'

She nodded. 'I had a word with his mother and she seems more relaxed.'

He nodded. 'Dealing with parents is a major part of our work.'

'I remember Vic telling me that.'

'And you haven't forgotten, have you?' he said softly. 'I saw you with Joey earlier. You relate well to everyone, whatever their age. Now, where are the notes of these you want me to take a look at?'

She sighed and handed them to him, then showed the first girl through to his room. She closed the door behind her thoughtfully. He seemed so down. Was it because he regretted the decision he had made the evening before? Or was he worried about Roger?

Pam beckoned her through for a cup of tea. 'Leave him to it. You've coped with the rest.'

Before they left Sara on call for the night, she was able to tell them that ventilation hadn't been necessary and that Roger's condition was improving.

The incident had pushed all thought of Gail's own problems to the back of her mind, but when she was alone in her room later that evening she thought again about what Sara had been saying.

Aware that it would be difficult to reopen the subject with her, her determination to quiz her mother was strengthened. By Friday she couldn't wait to get home.

She described her holiday in detail and showed her mother the photographs, then tried to broach the subject of her brother.

'Did you ever hear exactly what happened, Mum?'

'Of course I heard. I went to the inquest, didn't I? Matt ran off when your brother needed help. Haven't I told you that more than enough times?'

'Yes, you've told me, but somehow it doesn't seem the kind of thing Matt Roberts would do.'

'Maybe not now, but he did then. He's not trying to protest his innocence, is he?'

'No, Mum. He won't talk about it. But the new registrar was a medical student around the same time, and she suggests Matt told them a very different story at the time.'

'Well, he would, wouldn't he? Wouldn't want to lose face with his friends, would he?'

Gail sighed. 'I suppose not, but—'

'You're not going soft on him, are you? Because I can tell you, I won't have him in the house. As far as I'm concerned he's a murderer.'

'Mum! That's a dreadful thing to say.'

'I'm afraid that's what I believe. Now, let's forget all about it or we'll both have nightmares tonight.'

Gail realised there was nothing more she could do that evening, but she was determined to somehow ferret out the whole truth.

The next day she tried again. 'Were there any papers from the inquest, Mum?'

'If there were I've long since got rid of them.'

'Any newspaper reports?'

Her mother lost her temper. 'Are you doubting what I told you? Do you think I can't remember every single detail without bits of paper to prompt me? I can remember everything as clearly as if it happened yesterday—' she burst into tears '—and you of all people should know I don't want to think about it. Ever.'

Gail encircled her with her arms. 'I didn't mean to upset you, Mum,' she told her soothingly. 'I suppose I was only young at the time and didn't really know what was said. Please don't worry any more. It's not important.'

However, discovering the truth now assumed gigantic importance in Gail's mind. The moment she had a break on

Monday morning she rang the coroner's office and asked if there was any chance of her seeing the transcripts from an inquest.

'If you're a legitimate enquirer, certainly there is. Was the inquest held locally?'

'I think so. It was a skiing accident in France, but I'm sure I remember there was an inquest here.'

'There would be if this is where the funeral took place. But very often these cases from abroad will have taped evidence of the investigation as well. I expect we'll be able to find that for you. But you'll have to apply in writing.'

Gail used her lunch-hour to compose the letter and posted it in the front hall before returning for the asthma clinic.

She watched for the post every day and after two weeks rang the office again, only to be told they were very busy and she would hear as soon as they had a moment free.

'It wasn't needed urgently, was it?' the young girl at the other end of the telephone line asked.

Although she was desperate for the answer, Gail couldn't say it was urgent in the sense she meant.

Matt had been as good as his word and, although he helped her all he could in the clinics, she had not seen him at the gym and he had not suggested she join him, even for meals in the canteen.

When nothing had arrived from the coroner's office by Friday, she decided to visit the gym to work off her frustration.

Matt was in the exercise room. He seemed as uneasy as she was at the meeting, but they both relaxed as the evening progressed and enjoyed the swim that rounded off their exercise.

When Gail emerged from the changing room she saw that it was raining and she cursed that she hadn't checked the weather forecast before leaving the car behind.

'You can't walk home in this.'

The rain was certainly sheeting down and she accepted gratefully when he said, 'I'll run you back to the hospital.'

The moment there was a lull in the downpour, he took her arm and they splashed through the puddles to his car.

As he pulled out of the car park onto the main road Gail cried, 'Matt! There's a kiddie sitting on the pavement. What on earth is she doing? At least, I think it's a girl.'

Matt slowed down, but said, 'She's probably from one of the flats.'

'She's not old enough to be out there on her own, surely. Please stop, Matt. We can't leave her there. I'll go and see what's the matter.'

It wasn't easy on the busy road, but he found a place eventually.

Gail leapt from the car and raced back towards the soaking wet bundle who hadn't moved. Gail couldn't believe that people were just walking round her.

She bent down to speak to the child and saw with horror that she knew her.

'What on earth are you doing, Emma?'

The little girl looked up with tears joining the drips from her straggling wet hair. She wiped a soaking sleeve across her face, but didn't speak.

Matt had found a safe place to leave the car and came running towards them.

'It's Emma Langdon,' she told him quietly. 'We must get her home. Mrs G will be out of her mind with worry.'

Emma resisted all their attempts to get her onto her feet or to find out where she lived.

'Let us help you, Emma,' Gail coaxed. 'Your foster mother must wonder where you are. Is it far to the house?'

Emma didn't answer. Gail frowned towards Matt. 'Can we get the address from the hospital?'

'I think it's best if we leave this to the social services,' he told her quietly. 'First let's get her in the car and out of this rain.'

The hospital switchboard gave him the number for the duty social worker and he punched it out.

When there was no answer, he said to Gail, 'My flat's just round the corner. Let's get her into a warm bath. She's shivering.'

As he drove the short distance, Gail tried again to persuade Emma to tell them where she was living and what the problem was, but she merely shook her head and deliberately tightened her lips together.

Matt opened the door of his flat and stood back to allow Gail and Emma to enter. Gail saw it was definitely a luxury one and set Emma down to remove both their shoes and Emma's socks.

When he led the way through to the kitchen, they both followed. Gail was saddened to see the luxury decor and sumptuous furnishings without a single personal touch that made it into a home.

'Bath first?'

Gail nodded and he showed her the bathroom, found her a couple of clean towels and left her to run the bath while he tried to ring the social services again.

He must have been successful that time because she could hear him speaking, and unusually raising his voice.

He was clearly exasperated when he came up to join them, and motioned Gail out of Emma's hearing for a moment.

'Has she said anything?'

Gail shook her head.

'So much for trying to do things correctly. The social worker didn't want to know until I threatened to put Emma back where we found her. I'm tempted to try and get Mrs Grange's address from her hospital records after all.'

Gail tried not to grin.

'What did she say then?'

'She'll try and find out what's happened. She'll get back

to me but it could take a long time as she's snowed under with calls.'

'I can't put Emma back in her wet clothes.'

'Wrap her in a towel for now and I'll put the clothes in the tumble-dryer.'

When Gail joined him downstairs, he had made a cup of coffee for them both. He took Emma from her arms and placed her on the settee.

'Would you like a drink, Emma?'

The little girl shook her head.

'Something to eat?'

Another negative response.

He switched on the television in the corner and Gail was amused at him flicking through the channels until he found one he considered suitable for Emma.

'Gail and I are going to have a hot milky drink. What about you?'

Emma still shook her head and then uttered her first words since they had found her. 'I ain't going back.'

'Why ever not?' Gail asked quietly.

'She hates me.'

Presuming she was talking about Mrs Grange, Gail said, 'I can't believe that. She brought you to see us because she cared about you.'

Emma wrinkled her nose and turned her concentration to the television.

Matt raised his eyebrows in despair and then went through to the kitchen. 'Her clothes should be dry in a moment.'

'What then?'

'We can't do anything but wait. I'm sorry if I'm keeping you from anything, Gail, but I'd appreciate it if you would stay here until she's collected.'

She'd already worked out that she couldn't leave him alone with a young girl, but her heart still skipped a couple of beats as she murmured, 'No problem, Matt.'

The appreciative warmth of his smile enveloped her and she turned her head quickly to hide the tell-tale flush of colour staining her cheeks.

'Shall I phone for pizzas?'

'Would you like me to rustle something up for us all?'

'My housekeeper will have left me something to cook, but it'll only be enough for one and I doubt you'll find much else in the fridge.'

She felt a sudden heart-clenching pity for his way of life. Who was this girl who had broken his heart and reduced him to such a lonely existence? How could anyone be so cruel as to do that to someone like Matt?

CHAPTER NINE

THEY were so hungry by the time the pizzas arrived that they were enjoyed by them all. Even Emma.

She fell asleep on the settee almost immediately afterwards and they covered her with a blanket and adjourned to the kitchen.

'She certainly enjoyed that meal, didn't she?'

'Probably because we didn't have any of her enzymes or vitamins to give her with it,' Matt said ruefully. 'I only hope she doesn't suffer too much tomorrow.'

While he primed the coffee-maker, Gail rummaged through the freezer and the fridge. 'I can't find anything but fresh fruit for a dessert, not even—'

'You know, I'm not in the least sorry,' he whispered in her ear. She hadn't heard him come towards her and he took her by complete surprise when he pulled her into his arms. 'You're the only sweet course I'm remotely interested in. I was a fool to say I'd stop pestering you with invitations.'

Bending slightly, his lips met hers with a warm firmness that sent a myriad sensations flooding through her body. She could smell the fresh scent of his shower gel, but although it was a heady potion it was her own reaction that made her pull back from him sharply.

Until that moment she had believed she could handle them being cooped up together for a short time. She hadn't bargained for the unfamiliar turbulence that physical longing had aroused in her the moment their lips had touched.

'Gail, love—' his voice was tormented '—that was unforgivable of me, but I—I couldn't help myself.'

She reached out a hand to gently touch his arm and her voice trembled as she murmured, 'Neither could I.'

He groaned. 'I've tried so very hard to distance myself from you—'

'Please, Matt. I—'

'Before you say anything, let me finish, Gail, in case I lose my courage. I can't deny your repeated refusals of my invitations hurt, but I understand why you've been unable to accept. Which is all the more reason why I should have controlled myself a few moments ago, but the temptation was too great—my feelings for you are too strong. I was a fool to try and ignore them.'

'I understand, Matt,' she told him quietly.

'You do?'

She heard the incredulity and hope in his voice and knew that if she really did love him, then now was the time to forget her reservations and tell him so.

And she would have done so, if only he were free to love her, but... 'It's an artificial attraction, Matt. You feel sorry for me, that's all.'

'It's more than that, Gail. Much more, I promise you. But I had no right to act on it just because we're thrown together by unusual circumstances.'

She moved towards him and rested her hands on his upper arms, her emotions torn between her love for him and the knowledge that his heart belonged to another.

'Neither of us will ever be able to forget that George would be alive today but for my cowardice.'

'I don't believe you were responsible, Matt,' she told him quietly.

He stared at her disbelievingly, then blurted, 'However much we may want to, Gail, we can't dispute the truth.'

'I don't believe it is the truth, Matt.'

'Oh, Gail.' Almost unconsciously he pulled her closer. 'You are the kindest, most forgiving—'

She reached up and rested a finger over his lips, preventing him from continuing.

'Don't fool yourself. When I first came to Lizzie's, Matt, I hated you. I had been so brainwashed by my mother into despising you that I made up my mind to make life unbearable for you.'

'I can't believe—'

'I couldn't do it, Matt. The more I got to know you, the more impossible it became, until I got to the stage where I began to wonder if what I had always been told *was* the truth.'

'Oh, Gail—' his hold on her tightened and he cradled her head onto his shoulder, gently stroking her hair as he went on '—I don't deserve your trust. Maybe what your mother has always believed isn't altogether the truth, but it didn't matter, because *I* can never forgive myself—'

She sighed deeply and raised her eyes to search his face. 'I had a chat with Sara last week, Matt. She remembers you coming back and describing what happened. It doesn't tally with what Mum's always said.'

She felt him stir and looked up as he dropped a light kiss on her forehead. 'Gail, I barely knew Sara at that time. Neither did George.'

'I know. That's exactly what she told me.'

'So how could *she* know what happened?'

'She said learning that I was George's sister made her recall things she never realised she knew.'

He groaned and pulled her closer again. 'Gail, this is—'

The doorbell pealed, startling them both.

She moved away as Matt snatched up the remote entry handset and barked, 'Who is it?'

It was the social worker and she had so much to say that she didn't wait for him to release the door.

Matt raised an amused eyebrow in Gail's direction and interrupted the flow. 'Wouldn't it be better if you came up so that we could discuss this?'

Matt went through to open the flat door and Gail switched the kettle on. When she'd been introduced she asked, 'Would you like a cup of coffee, Tania?'

'That would be very nice, thanks. I haven't had a moment.'

When they were all seated round the kitchen table with their coffee, she told them, 'Emma has been living with a foster mother. She's reluctant to take her back.'

'Why?' Matt asked.

'There appears to have been a gradual breaking down which came to a head this evening.'

'So, where will she go?'

'That's the problem. Normally we'd find her a place in a children's home or an emergency foster home for the night, but it's not proving easy and it's getting late. Emma's already sleeping. I know it's an imposition, but as you two know her, and are both professionals, would it be possible for her to stay here the night? I've collected her medication and a few of her clothes from Mrs Grange.'

Matt glanced across at Gail. 'Dr Peters doesn't actually live here. She's a colleague from work. I was giving her a lift home from the gym because it was raining.' Tania looked from one to the other, clearly finding his explanation hard to believe, and Gail cursed the flush that she knew was highlighting her cheeks.

'If it'll help, I'll stay tonight,' she told them, checking her watch. 'What's left of it.'

Tania was clearly grateful. 'Someone will contact you first thing in the morning, I promise.'

'If the weekend duty officer can find her a place,' Matt muttered when he returned from showing Tania out. 'I'll stay up in case Emma wakes.' He seemed suddenly uneasy, unsure of how to handle the unexpected situation they found themselves in.

'There's a bed—'

'Do you—?' They both started to speak at once.

'After you.' He laughed.

'I was about to ask if you'd like another coffee.' She wanted to resume the evening where it had been so cruelly interrupted.

'And I was about to say there's a bed made up in the spare room.'

'Coffee first?'

He nodded.

When she handed him his, he grimaced. 'Kitchen seats are all right, but a bit of comfort wouldn't come amiss, would it?'

She took a deep breath. 'Matt, about George—'

'No, Gail.' He leaned across and took both her hands in his and kissed each of them in turn. 'You're a lovely girl and if only things were different—'

'But they are, Matt,' she cried out. 'At least they could be. Don't you see? Knowing the truth will help us both to remember the happy times with George—not the bitterness and acrimony that has existed between us up to now.'

Matt shook his head, then said quietly, 'It's too late, Gail.'

'Please share with me what exactly happened, Matt. I want to hear—'

A piercing scream from the living room drowned out the rest of her words. They both leapt to their feet and raced through to find Emma sobbing.

Gail wrapped her arms around her. 'It's all right. Emma. You're safe here. Did you have a bad dream?'

Emma seemed to have forgotten her resolve not to speak. 'It was horrible. He hit me again and again.'

Gail whispered, 'Who hit you, Emma?'

'Jeremy. He said I was pretending to be ill so as I could take his mum from him.'

Remembering Emma dealing roughly with the two bigger boys in front of the fish tank, Gail was surprised that she hadn't retaliated. Wasn't Jeremy only seven? Perhaps she had! But now was not the time to try and find out.

'I need to go to the toilet,' Emma confided to Gail.

She reminded her where it was and closed the door. Matt, who had been hovering in the background, queried, 'Pizza upsetting her, perhaps?'

Gail shrugged. 'Probably. At least we've got her medication now.'

He nodded. 'And some clean clothes. I hope it doesn't mean they are going to forget about her until Monday.'

Privately Gail thought it might be a good thing if they did! She and Matt might have sorted a few things out between them by that time!

When the little girl reappeared, Gail offered her a drink, which she refused. 'We'll make you comfortable in Dr Roberts' spare bed for the night.'

Matt started, 'But—'

Gail shook her head to silence him and smiled.

When Emma had eventually settled, he said, 'I meant that bed for you.'

'She needed it more. I'll be all right on the settee.'

'We'll see about that.' He poured their cold coffee away and made some more, but this time they carried it through to the living area.

'You were about to tell me what happened to George,' Gail prompted.

'I'm not sure that I was—perhaps Emma's interruption was meant to remind me it's not a good idea.'

'Why?'

'It could make the situation even worse.'

'How? Please, Matt,' she pleaded. 'I have to know if Sara had it right.'

'I suppose…' He sighed. 'George was a fine fellow, Gail—'

'I know that.'

'He was a great friend and we did most things together.'

She nodded. 'I remember.'

'But that day it was different.'

She frowned. 'Different in what way?'

'I don't know. Well, I do, but I don't know why I didn't want to go with him.'

'You're talking in riddles, Matt?'

'George loved taking risks, Gail. So did I. We thought we were infallible. I was just as bad as him. But for some reason that day I thought it was one risk too many.'

Gail held her breath.

'We knew there was a warning not to ski off-piste but George was determined to do so. He was convinced he knew better.'

'But you weren't.'

'I chickened out that day.'

'Did you know—?'

'I was frightened. And I told George that I thought it was one day we should obey the rules. Don't ask me why. To this day I don't know, but I had this gut feeling. I thought if I refused to go with him he wouldn't go either, but he found someone else willing to take the risk.

'I watched them leave, then decided to go after them. I was worried about what George might do if I wasn't there.

'But I had to get ready and was still quite a way behind when the avalanche struck. It missed me by inches, but I saw your brother and his companion swept off their feet in front of the wall of snow.'

He buried his face in his hands. 'It took me too long to reach them. If I'd been right behind I could perhaps have pulled them clear before the second wave of snow claimed them.'

She took him in her arms and tried to comfort him, almost as she had done Emma.

'I raised the alarm then tried to dig them out. But I had nothing but my bare hands and it took too long.' He shuddered at the memory.

'You *can't* blame yourself, Matt,' she told him quietly. 'George was old enough to make his own decisions. You weren't his nursemaid.' She felt a sudden flash of anger towards her brother for causing Matt so much grief through his own stupidity.

Tears flowed down her cheeks, and Matt tightened his hold on her and murmured, 'I'm sorry, Gail. I knew this would be a mistake…'

She struggled to speak through her sobs. 'I idolised George. Always believed he could do no wrong. I was so wrong, almost as stupid as him. I should have known better—'

'You were so young, Gail. And I can understand how your mother feels. In her heart of hearts she probably knew what George was like, but she doesn't want your memory of him tarnished.'

'But it wouldn't have been,' Gail cried. 'It's headstrong characters like him, willing to take risks, who make the spectacular advances in this world. OK, this time it didn't come off, but he could have made a real difference to the medical world.'

When her sobs began to subside, he gently wiped away her tears, then his lips met hers, comforting and healing with what Gail now hoped was a promise for the future. A promise that Matt, in time, could forget his earlier heartbreak and fulfil her dreams that had started over ten years earlier.

When they broke apart, as the need to breathe decreed they must, Gail felt bereft and reached out to hold him close, sure that he couldn't help but be affected by similar exquisite sensations.

Watching her through eyelids heavy with desire, he slid a warm hand inside the opening of her sports shirt. Every nerve-ending in her body was sensitised to his touch, making it impossible for her to resist, even if she had wanted to, and she knew in that moment she didn't.

'Gail,' he breathed, as his fingers moved to the tip of one of her firm breasts, filling her with an overwhelming longing.

She barely noticed the deft movement of his other hand as it moved to slide her cotton top over her head, exposing both unclad breasts to his darkening gaze. 'You're so beautiful,' he whispered. 'And so, so tempting.' He buried his head between the softness and as she lightly caressed the back of his head and his neck, her whole body alive with a new awareness of him, she was shocked to feel a wetness that could only be his tears.

'Matt, love,' she whispered. 'What on earth's the matter?'

He raised his head and murmured, 'You're so lovely, Gail, and I want you desperately, but it can never be.'

With shaking hands he slipped her shirt back over her head again and hugged her to him. 'Why is fate so cruel?'

'I—I don't understand, Matt…' She was bewildered by his words as she struggled to free herself from the emotions he had aroused within her.

'I'm sorry, Gail.' He moved right away from her then and said dispassionately, 'You can sleep in my bed tonight. Mrs C will have changed the sheets today. I'll stay here.'

'I'll be more comfortable on the settee than you would be with your great length,' she murmured lightly in the hope of rekindling the charged atmosphere of a few moments before. 'Unless—' she added suggestively.

'No, Gail,' he broke in urgently. 'I was wrong to start something that could never be—'

'You seemed happy enough when you were undressing me.'

'I *was* happy, Gail, until I remembered your mother.'

'My mother?'

'The last thing I want to do is alienate you from her.'

'Alienate me?' She was so bewildered that she knew she must sound like a parrot repeating his words.

'It would mean you making a choice between me and your mother, and that would make you unhappy. Something I couldn't bear. You would come to hate me.'

Raking her fingers distractedly through her hair, she muttered, 'Why on earth should it mean a choice?'

'Gail, you know as well as I do how she feels about me. *You* might now accept the truth of what happened all those years ago, but she has known it all along. And refused to believe it. Would she believe now that her precious son could have contributed to his own death by his foolhardiness? Be truthful, she would never accept me as your lover, would she?'

Lover. Was that all he would be offering? With a sickening jolt, she recalled Sara telling her that if he couldn't marry the girl he really loved, he wouldn't make do with second best. Was that what she was? Second best?

How convenient to use her mother as the excuse for his lack of commitment. She moved angrily to the other side of the room.

'Your lover?' she muttered scathingly. 'No. I don't suppose she would. When you vacate the settee, I'll get my head down, thanks. Goodnight, Matt.'

'Gail!' His tone was pleading. 'You've no idea how much I wish things could be different.'

'Oh, but I have, Matt,' she muttered bitterly. 'Believe me, I have.'

He came across and tried to grasp her arms. 'Please, Gail.'

She shrugged him away. 'I don't want to discuss it any further, Matt. I'd be grateful for a blanket, though.'

He went through to his bedroom and returned with a duvet. Handing it to her, he tried again to speak to her, but she resolutely refused to listen. 'Please, Matt. I need my sleep. Goodnight.'

He searched her face for several long moments, then,

shaking his head, left the room, closing the door behind him.

She subsided onto the makeshift bed, no longer able to cry. Over the months they'd been working together, she'd sensed an empathy developing and had believed that George's death was all that stood between them. It hurt and hurt badly that, now the truth had resolved that problem, Matt wanted nothing more than an affair.

Gail found sleep elusive that night, but she was so emotionally exhausted that she must have dropped into a deep sleep as dawn was tingeing the sky.

She was woken by Matt answering the doorbell and asking whoever had called to come up. Checking her watch, she saw it was just before nine. She leapt from the settee and crept through to the bathroom, thankful to meet no one on the way.

When she emerged, Matt and Emma were in the living room miraculously cleared of Gail's bedding. Matt introduced her to Diane, Emma's usual social worker.

'Tania rang me for advice and, as I know her so well—' she smiled at Emma '—I offered to make the new arrangements for her.

'I do want to thank you both for taking such good care of her. I've just been explaining to her that we've found her a place to stay for the time being.'

Emma was seated sullenly on the settee and Gail felt her heart breaking at the thought of yet another temporary home for her. She knew exactly how Emma must feel. It was bad enough knowing Matt didn't want her. How much more must Emma be suffering to know that nobody at all wanted *her*? It didn't bear thinking about.

Gail moved to her side. Emma slipped a hand into hers. 'Can't I stay here?'

Diane answered before Gail had a chance. 'Of course not. They've been very kind looking after you overnight and giving you breakfast, especially when you've been so naughty—'

Gail flashed a guilty look towards Matt. He must have been up early with Emma and she hadn't heard a thing.

'I wasn't naughty. I wasn't naughty. It was Jeremy.' Emma was becoming distressed and Gail wanted to give her a consoling hug, but wasn't sure how Diane would react.

'Just say thank you, Emma, and we'll leave these nice people to their weekend.'

Emma mumbled the words truculently and Diane took her hand firmly, pulling her from beside Gail.

'We'll see you soon at the clinic,' Matt told her as he showed them out of the door, but Emma didn't look back.

Gail tried to prevent the tears spilling from her eyes, and went in search of her jacket.

Matt took it from her. 'Have some breakfast before you go.'

She shook her head.

'At least a cup of coffee?'

She reluctantly agreed.

'You gave Emma breakfast?'

He nodded. 'I managed that.'

'I'm sorry. I didn't hear you about. I didn't sleep all that well.'

He shrugged. 'Don't say I didn't warn you.'

She tried to smile. 'It wasn't the settee. I was worrying about Emma.'

He touched her arm. 'I know, Gail. So was I.'

He went through to the kitchen to make the coffee.

'Have you plans for the rest of the day?' he asked when he returned.

'I'm supposed to be meeting a friend for lunch.' She checked her watch. 'Jeepers. I'd better get a move on if I'm to get home and change and be there on time.'

'You're welcome to ring, if it'll help,' he offered.

She hurriedly drained her cup. 'Thanks, Matt, but I don't have her number with me.'

'I'll run you to Lizzie's.'

'It'll be as quick to walk from here, Matt, thanks.'

She grabbed her jacket and he accompanied her to the door.

'Thanks for staying the night,' he told her. 'See you Monday, no doubt.'

She nodded and walked off quickly in the direction of the hospital, asking herself how they could have descended into conversing so formally after what had happened the evening before. As if she didn't know. The answer pounded through her head in time with her footsteps. All he wanted was an affair.

Gail scrambled into the Monday morning clinic as the first patients were arriving.

'Heavy weekend?' Betty teased cheerfully.

Gail shook her head. 'I haven't been sleeping too well recently.'

Sara joined them. 'Worrying if you're making the right move for your career?'

Gail tried to smile reassuringly. 'No, I'm looking forward to getting right away from London. Should be quite an experience for me.' She laughed. 'That must sound daft to someone who's been over to the other side of the world to work!'

'Perhaps that's where you're destined for next.'

'I don't know about that.' Gail checked her watch. 'Have I time to go up and check if they need anything on the unit before I'm needed here?'

Sara shook her head. 'I've already been up and also seen young Roger who's been transferred from ITU. He should be able to go home tomorrow. I need your help here at the moment. Matt won't be in until later.'

Gail jerked her head up in surprise. 'Why's that?'

Betty giggled. 'Perhaps he's not been sleeping too well either.'

Sara joined in the laughter, then said, 'I don't really know. He just asked if I could cope for a couple of hours.'

Sara must have sensed Gail's unhappiness the moment she walked into the department, and over coffee she tried to probe for a reason, but Gail didn't want to talk about it.

She knew Matt had arrived in the department, but deliberately kept herself busy so that she couldn't join him and Sara for lunch when she asked.

When she collected her mail at lunch-time, there was a large envelope from the coroner's office.

She cast it aside unopened. What a waste of effort wading through all that bureaucratic nonsense! She already knew the truth and it hadn't made the slightest bit of difference. What a fool she had been to ever believe it could.

She returned to the clinic. She enjoyed Monday afternoons. Asthma was still the chest condition she knew most about and seeing the improvement in so many of the children once a correct therapeutic drug routine was established made her feel she'd achieved something worthwhile.

With so many of the children referred to Lizzie's, helping them was as simple as teaching them to use their various inhalers properly. Or emphasising the importance of regular usage.

The most rewarding were those who attended for several weeks until exactly the right combination of medication allowed them to lead a nearly normal life. It was a revelation to many of them that they could exercise and take part in games. Her last patient, Ryan Walker, was one of those.

He had attended the clinic for many months before his asthma had been sufficiently controlled for him to be able to play football. Now he was a member of the school team.

Unfortunately he seemed prone to chest infections and these quickly tipped his asthma out of control, as Gail well remembered from her early days in the unit. But in between he could play the game he loved.

The boy came in with his father as usual. 'Take a seat,' she told them both. 'Let's see, it's six weeks since you were last with us, isn't it? How have you been?'

'Fine.'

'Footballing.'

The boy looked at his father. 'We've finished for the summer.'

'Are you doing some other sport in its place?'

'Dad won't let me.'

Mr Walker looked sheepish. 'He did want to take up horse riding. Considering the results of his allergy tests, I didn't think it a good idea.'

She checked the results of the skin tests and saw that, as well as the house-dust mite, animals were the biggest problem for Ryan.

She smiled. 'I think I agree with that. Have you thought about joining a gym, Ryan?'

The boy shook his head but looked interested.

'Perhaps you could give one a try.'

She turned to his father. 'These days gyms have fitness experts who will take into account his asthma and work out a programme especially for him. It could do him a lot of good, especially if he can swim, and it'll keep him in good shape for his football.'

Matt came in search of her as she saw Ryan out. 'You look better,' he told the boy.

Gail told him she had suggested Ryan try a gym for the summer and Matt endorsed the idea.

When they had left the department, he followed Gail back into her room and closed the door.

'I thought you'd like to know that I went to a meeting about Emma this morning.'

She was surprised. 'A case conference? Why not her GP?'

'It was more informal than that and anyway she has just moved out of yet another GP's catchment area. They asked if I could fill them in on the details of her illness.'

'So where is she now?'

'With a couple who specialise in emergency care in cases like this.'

'Poor girl—'

'She's apparently happy there. So far!'

'But it's only temporary,' she blurted out miserably. 'If only they could find her somewhere more settled—'

'She doesn't help herself, Gail,' he told her quietly. 'She can be very difficult.'

She glared at him. 'What chance has she had to learn to behave any differently? She needs someone who really cares about her.'

'Don't forget Mrs Grange was concerned enough to bring her to see us.'

'I suppose so, but her son didn't like it, did he?'

'No, I admit it's probably not always Emma's fault that her placements don't work, but—'

'How can people like you and I who come from loving homes ever know what it's like?' she demanded ferociously.

He regarded her steadily for a few moments. '*You* may have come from a loving home, Gail. *I* am the product of a succession of foster homes. Until the accident, your mother was the nearest thing to a parent I ever had.'

CHAPTER TEN

GAIL groaned. 'Oh, Matt! I'd no idea.' That was why he'd been at their home so much as a student. It hadn't really occurred to her before but now it started to make sense. He'd had no home of his own to go to in the university vacations. How little she really knew about this man she believed she loved.

She felt dreadful. Until she'd come to Lizzie's she hadn't given a thought to how George's death had affected Matt, but it hadn't taken her long to learn. Now she could see how much worse it must have been for him. How rejected he must have felt by her mother's attitude. 'Matt, I'm so sorry. That was thoughtless of me.' No wonder he was so sympathetic towards Emma.

'You weren't to know,' he reassured her with a smile. 'It was all a long time ago. Anyway, that wasn't what I came to talk about. I've an idea about Emma's future which I'd like to discuss with you before I speak to anyone else.' He checked his watch. 'But I have a meeting now.'

'Tomorrow?'

He was hesitant. 'I don't really want to leave it that long. How about us meeting up this evening if I pick you up about seven-thirty? Perhaps we could talk over a meal— something better than a pizza?'

She was torn. Between not wanting to cause him any more hurt after all he had been through, and keeping her own heart from breaking completely. 'I'm afraid I'm on call this evening.'

'I'll have my mobile,' he told her hopefully.

She hesitated, but told herself he only wanted to meet her for a discussion about Emma's future. If he had found a way that might change it for the better, it would be unfair to the little girl to refuse to do anything she could to help.

After all the problems there had been, she could see why he wanted to try his idea out on her before putting it forward to the authorities. She owed it to Emma to at least listen to what he had to say.

He looked at his watch again. 'Gail—'

'OK. Seven-thirty it is, but I don't want to be back late.'

'Thanks, love. I appreciate that.' He rushed from the room, leaving her shaken at the effect his throwaway endearment could have on her.

She hadn't moved when he popped his head round the door a few moments later and told her, 'Just to let you know I've booked a table at Anton's to make up for that pizza. *Ciao.*' He was gone again before she could protest.

She knew why he had said it. Anton's was the dressiest, most expensive restaurant in town. He hadn't wanted her turning up in jeans!

Grateful that he had told her, she made her way back to her room wondering what she could wear. He probably didn't go there very often and she wanted to look her best for him. He worked so hard that he deserved more such outings, but, since her advent in the department and Vic's departure, she knew they had been few and far between.

The unopened package from the coroner was the first thing she saw when she opened the door of her room, and her curiosity got the better of her. Had he really told her the truth, the whole truth and nothing but the truth?

When she did eventually open the envelope, it was with trembling fingers.

She found a photocopied transcript of the inquest result and an invitation to hear the taped evidence that had come from the enquiry abroad.

As she read, it became clear that Matt had described exactly the events of that day and her heart bled for him.

The scene must be imprinted on his memory and her probing for the truth must have brought it back into sharp focus.

It was too late now. The damage was done. She only hoped he would be able to forget the worst memories once she had left the department. She dressed carefully, settling on a deep pink dress and jacket and strappy sandals, and was ready when he arrived to pick her up. He was wearing a smartly tailored deep blue suit that, with the lighter blue shirt he was wearing, made him seem more attractive than ever to Gail.

'You look—um—special,' he greeted her, eyeing her dress with obvious approval.

Trying to convince herself that this was nothing more than a business meeting, she struggled to ignore the lurch that twisted her heart when he took her arm, but she knew it was an impossibility and that she should never have agreed to join him for the evening, whatever his excuse.

Because she loved him, so much that she just knew it would result in her hurting even more at the end of it.

Anton showed them through to a secluded table and asked if they would like aperitifs.

At Matt's querying eyebrow she ordered a plain tonic water.

He shook his head. 'You can drink. Sara's doing your on-call.'

She started to protest.

'She didn't mind. She wasn't doing anything else. Now, gin in that tonic all right?'

She nodded in bewilderment. 'But—'

'Make that two,' he told the waiter.

She was surprised. On their other outings he'd rarely drunk alcohol, as he'd been driving, and she guessed he would limit himself to that one. So she was surprised when he ordered a couple of bottles from the wine list, ordering them by number. 'I'll tell you when we want the second one opened,' he told the wine waiter.

They perused the menus silently, Gail trying unsuccessfully to fathom why on earth he had bothered to change her on-call duty.

After they had ordered, he lifted his drink which had arrived a moment earlier and toasted, 'To the future. Whatever it might bring.'

Gail joined him, presuming he was talking about Emma. 'So tell me. What is your plan?' she asked him.

'That would be telling,' he teased.

'I meant your plan for Emma's future,' she muttered somewhat testily. 'I thought that was what we had come to discuss.'

'All in good time. I think we need some food inside us first.' As if at his command, the starters arrived at that moment.

Gail had chosen a deep-fried soft cheese with gooseberry sauce and it was delicious, as was Matt's choice of 'saucy' seafood in a filo pastry case.

While they waited for their main courses, their wineglasses were filled with a deep red wine, Matt having had a taster first.

He raised his glass again. 'To *our* futures this time.'

She joined him in the toast, but then asked suspiciously, 'But what about Emma's?'

'As I said before, all in good time!' He smiled and reached across the table to catch one of her hands in his own, throwing her into a confusion that she knew must be obvious in her burning cheeks.

Their main dishes were served then, but when she pushed her plate away, leaving more than she had eaten, she could not have said what it was she had ordered, because Matt's inscrutable behaviour was making her uneasy. He seemed almost to have reverted to the carefree student she had known all those years ago, lightening her own heart in the process.

He enjoyed every morsel of food on his plate and when

he laid down his knife and fork he murmured, 'That was fantastic. But yours wasn't?'

Her heart delighted by his obvious enjoyment, she told him, 'It was lovely. I just don't have such a big appetite any more.'

She saw he had refilled her glass without her noticing and he leaned back in his chair and raised his own while watching her with smiling eyes. 'This time, Gail, I think we'll drink to our future *together*.'

This time she didn't join him in the toast. When she looked up and met his eyes watching her with amusement, it seemed as if time stood still and all the while her heart flipped over and over, matching the soft, seductive beat of the music that had washed over them unnoticed since they had entered the restaurant.

He leaned forward and reached across the table to this time catch hold of both of her hands.

'I'm asking you to marry me, Gail. I love you, have always loved you since the day I first saw you and I always will love you.'

He lifted both her hands to his lips and when he lowered them he told her, 'It took our brief encounter on Friday evening to make me realise what I fool I've been. I've only ever wanted your happiness and I was going totally the wrong way about it.

'I know now that we're not meant to be apart. I've struggled to ignore how I felt for your sake, but now, deep in my heart, I know that together we'd be able to overcome each and every obstacle that stands in our way.' Tightening his hold on her hands, he whispered huskily, 'I'm just sorry, love, that it took me so long to recognise the truth.'

Overwhelmed by the sensations flooding through her, she neither spoke nor moved for several moments, then, making a huge effort, she stuttered, 'B-but, Matt... You said...' She shook her head as if to try and clear the fog. 'Wh-what about...?' Again she couldn't finish.

'Your mother?' he queried. 'I know we have a big problem there…'

She shook her head, then changed it to a nod, then blurted out, 'The girl who broke your heart. Sara told me about her.'

He didn't answer immediately and her heart dropped like a leaden weight. Then he started to laugh and it was so infectious that she had to join him, but her laughter was soon perilously close to tears.

Noticing, he sobered immediately and told her quietly, 'You little goose. It was *you* I was talking about,' he told her quietly.

'Me? But…' She felt more and more like Alice in an alien world. 'But I never—'

'I didn't mean you personally broke my heart. But however hard I tried I couldn't forget you and never expected you to ever look twice at me. Oh, Gail, I think I'm beginning to understand why you've given me the cold shoulder for so long. And I thought it was because of your mother.'

It was Gail's turn to laugh then. 'And I thought you were using my mother as an excuse not to make a commitment to me!'

'I suppose I was, in a way,' he told her seriously, 'but only because I was afraid you would be unhappily torn between love for each of us and I couldn't bear that to happen. I couldn't stand the thought of you hating me. But when you walked away on Saturday morning, I knew I couldn't live without you and that somehow, as long as we were together, we would find a solution.'

'Oh, Matt…' She had to swallow hard at the lump in her throat before she could say almost inaudibly, 'I love you, too, Matt.'

'This certainly calls for our second bottle.' He beckoned to the waiter, who brought champagne in an ice bucket.

When it had been opened and poured and the waiter had

discreetly disappeared, he murmured, 'To us, Gail. For ever and ever.'

This time she repeated the words and sipped the champagne with misty eyes. 'Oh, Matt. I've loved you for just as long as you've loved me.'

Tears began to cascade down her cheeks and he told her gently, 'I think it's time we found somewhere more congenial.'

'But, Matt—' she wiped away her tears '—you wanted to discuss Emma.'

'All in good time,' he told her with a wicked grin.

'You used Emma as a lure to get me here, didn't you? You never had a plan.' Her voice was rising accusingly.

'I did, and I have. All will be revealed later.'

He beckoned to Anton, who nodded and presented the bill. When they stepped outside, there was a cream stretch limousine awaiting them. 'But—but, your car, Matt.'

'I'll collect it in the morning.'

'But I can't arrive back at the residency in this.'

He grinned again, even more wickedly than before. 'You have a choice—either we roll up in the stretch limo at the hospital or you spend another night at my flat—this time in my bed!'

He took her arm and helped her inside and Anton closed the door, after passing in the champagne in its bucket and saying with a satisfied smile, 'Goodnight, sir, madam.'

The car purred into motion and Matt took her in his arms and his lips met hers with the gentle assurance of love. They were warm and firm and when Gail unconsciously returned the pressure she felt the moist sweetness of his tongue persuading her lips to open and a helplessness overwhelmed her. She became suddenly conscious that the purring of the engine had ceased, and put her hands on his chest to warn him that they were under the light outside his block of flats.

He smiled and looked down at her, his eyes dark with desire. 'It's not a crime to kiss my future wife.'

He released her and Gail, completely disorientated by the wonder of him calling her his future wife, climbed unsteadily from the car after him.

After a couple of words with the driver, Matt lifted out the champagne and, with his other arm drawing her close, they made their way up to his flat.

He put the ice bucket carefully down, unlocked the door and, sweeping her up into his arms, carried her over the threshold and onto his bed.

She turned and raised herself on one elbow and with a contented lethargy watched him retrieve the champagne, close the door and, lifting a couple of glasses on the way, join her in the bedroom.

He poured the champagne, then joined her on the bed, and, handing her a glass, said, 'I believe you wanted an early night, didn't you? Let's drink to our first night together, love.'

Later, much later, she stirred and murmured, 'You still haven't told me your plan for Emma.'

'Not told you, but allowed it to unfold. I thought when we are married, we might try to provide a home for her.'

'Oh, Matt. What a good idea. We—'

'It might not work,' he broke in hurriedly. 'The social workers might oppose it and even if they don't there's no guarantee she'll agree to live with us, and it'll mean a lot of work for us both—'

'And we might have children of our own,' she told him, tracing her finger lightly round his bare chest, 'I—I think I'd like that very much, as long as she was happy, but, Matt?'

'Yes?'

'What about my mother?'

He didn't answer immediately, then sighed deeply and said, 'Your mother has never listened, or at least never taken in what was being said. I walked away from you both because I thought contact with me was preventing her getting over her grief.

'I've thought a lot about her since Saturday, because it's clear from what you told me that she still won't let go.' He took her in her arms and kissed her gently before saying, 'And I know you're going to hate me for saying this, but I think she needs help. Professional help.'

'A psychiatrist?' Gail breathed.

'Not necessarily. There are some very good bereavement counsellors.' He hesitated, then said quietly, 'But there is one other way we might be able to convince her.'

Gail frowned, wondering if she should tell him about the papers from the coroner.

'I think, love, that the threat of you being unhappy, or even losing you if she doesn't accept me, might just be—'

'I couldn't do that to her, Matt,' Gail cried, pushing herself right away from him. 'It would be cruel.'

'Do you think she's happy at the moment, harbouring such bitterness all the time?'

'Well, no, I suppose not. I've often wished there was some way she could be persuaded to concentrate on her happy memories of George instead.'

'There you are, then.'

'I think I've a better idea. When you wouldn't talk about what happened, I applied to the coroner's office for a transcript of the inquest.'

'You did what?' Matt was incredulous. 'Why?'

'Because when I'd worked for you for only a short time, I couldn't believe you would walk away and leave anyone who needed help, and—'

He moved closer and encircled her again with his arms. 'Oh, Gail, love. I—I—' He was so overcome with emotion he had to struggle to finish. 'Thank you, thank you for believing in me.'

'The papers came today, and they confirm everything

happened exactly as you told me the other day. I—I'd like
to show them to Mum before I say anything about us.
Please?'

'She's your mother. If you think you can convince her—'

'She'll be your mother-in-law,' she teased.

'I'd like to think of her as my mother, as I used to do
before all this happened,' he told her quietly.

Gail smiled warmly as he pulled her back into his arms.
'I'm sure you'll be able to win her round, as you've done
me.'

'Not quite in the same way.' He grinned, before silencing
her answer with his lips.

'Come on, sleepyhead. Time to get Cinderella back to her
room before the gossips are about.'

Gail turned over and saw that it was nearly seven. 'Ugh.
I don't feel as if I've slept at all.'

'I don't think you have. Much!' he teased, handing her
a mug of coffee. 'Do you want breakfast?'

'No! I'll get something later.' She rolled off the bed and
searched for her clothes before making for the bathroom.

'Don't be long. There's a taxi on its way.'

When she emerged from the bathroom, she saw Matt was
already dressed for work.

Seeing her surprise, he told her, 'We'll get the taxi to
drop you at the hospital then go on to pick up my car.
There's no point in me coming home again.'

He put his arm round her in the taxi. 'Still happy?'

She nodded. 'I love you, Matt,' she told him before leap-
ing from the vehicle and managing to get to her room without being seen.

Not that it mattered. When she arrived just in time for
the start of the cystic fibrosis clinic, she discovered Matt
had lost no time in telling the whole department that they
were engaged.

'We told you so,' Pam and Betty chorused in unison and

both hugged her warmly. 'We expect an invite to the wedding.'

When Gail could eventually escape to her own consulting room, Sara walked with her. 'I'm so pleased for you both, Gail. It never for one minute occurred to me you were the girl he loved but couldn't have. I'm sorry if I put my foot completely in it. I couldn't have got it more wrong, could I?'

Gail grinned happily. 'No more than I did! I thought you were after him when you first came here.'

Sara laughed. 'I *was* a little jealous of you when I first started here. But only because you'd been working so closely with Matt that I thought he believed you the better doctor. I just know you're both going to be wildly happy. And I do wish you the best of luck. Believe me, taking on someone like Emma Langdon won't be easy.'

Gail smiled her thanks. 'I think I'm just beginning to realise that.'

But as she made her way into her own consulting room, she muttered to herself, 'But it'll be a hell of a lot easier than breaking the news about Matt to my mother!'

Matt came in search of her when it was time for lunch and, finding her alone in the room, he leant across the desk and kissed her.

'Regretting it yet?' he asked as he slumped into the nearest chair with a grin.

'I haven't had a moment to consider!' she teased, easing her own chair back into a more comfortable position.

'Finished your list?'

She nodded. 'Just completed the last notes.'

'Lunch, then.'

'What's happening on the unit?'

'Sara's got that under control. She'll join us in the dining room.'

As Gail stood and collected her records together, Matt

said seriously, 'There is something I need to get off my chest before we join the others.'

She sank back into her chair. What now? George? Or her mother again? 'Confession time?' She laughed lightly to cover her apprehension.

'Nothing like that, you little goose. It's your career. I don't want you haring off to Lancashire, so…'

'Yes?' Gail prompted suspiciously.

'I've spoken to Graham Wilson at St John's and they have an SHO job going which is yours if you want it.'

Gail looked at him aghast. 'St John's? I'm nowhere near experienced enough for a specialist heart hospital, and anyway—'

Matt raised a hand to silence her protests. 'They don't have pre-registration house officers, Gail, so you could be doing a lot of work usually done by juniors. But…' he rushed on persuasively '…if you don't mind that it'll be fantastic experience and look great on your CV.'

Gail was stunned by the unexpected offer. 'Do—do you know Graham well?'

He grinned. 'Well enough for him to agree to be my best man.'

'I—I—do you think it's a good idea for me to work with him, then?'

'The firms there are much larger than ours. You probably won't have much contact with the top man, but I consider you're more than capable to handle the work.'

She had to blink back the tears at his compliment and swallowed hard.

'I wasn't sure if you'd already accepted the Lancashire post.'

'No. I haven't completed the application form yet but…'

Matt leapt to his feet and, grabbing her round the waist, swung her off her feet. 'Thank goodness for that.'

When she'd steadied herself she told him sternly, 'Not so fast, Matt. I don't want to advance my career because your friends are doing you a favour. I want to do it on merit.'

'I know, love, and you will be. I'd be giving the reference for you.'

He took her hand. 'I'm sorry if I've overstepped the mark, but Lancashire's so far away and I was so hoping we could get married when you finish your stint here. I don't want to wait.'

He looked so comically penitent that she couldn't help laughing and moved to plant a kiss on his lips. 'I forgive you this time, but in future I'd prefer to organise my own career moves.'

'I'll remember.' He hugged her to him. 'How soon can we marry?'

'For Emma's sake…'

'For my sake!'

'For Emma's sake,' she reiterated firmly. 'I agree it'll be better sooner rather than later, so I'd thought about the first weekend in September.'

'September? That's over two months away!'

'It's not going to be an easy time and, anyway, I want to savour these weeks of getting to know you. And I'm just beginning to realise how much I don't know!' She kissed him gently. 'Some things just can't be hurried! And we have Mum to convince first, remember?'

'Only too well,' he told her ruefully. 'OK. I can see you've made up your mind so it's a date, but I refuse to wait a moment longer. Come on now. Let's eat.'

The break passed far too quickly in a flurry of congratulations and good luck wishes that barely left them time to eat their lunch.

As they walked back to the clinic Gail murmured, 'If we invite everyone who's expressed an interest, there won't be room for us at the wedding!'

'That's the beauty of working in a hospital. Most of them won't be able to get off duty, thank goodness.'

'That's a wicked thing to say, Matt Roberts! Betty and Pam will definitely be there and hopefully Sara. You should have a new SHO to hold the fort by that time.' She laughed. 'You knew them first so they can all fill the groom's side of the church. Together with Joy—and perhaps Monica.'

'You're so thoughtful.'

Ignoring his sarcasm, she changed the subject. 'I was wondering whether Emma might like to be my bridesmaid.'

'What a great idea. She'd love that.'

'Have you said anything about our idea to Diane yet?'

'I spoke to her earlier. She thinks it might work. To start with Emma would be allowed out for days with us. If it looks like it's working, Diane's promised she won't be moved on for the moment.'

'Let's hope it does for Emma's sake.'

'If you agree, I thought Sunday might be a good day to start.'

'Sounds fine to me.'

Before they pushed their way through the doors to the waiting room he kissed her. 'We'll hunt for that special engagement ring everyone keeps asking to see on Saturday.'

She shook her head. 'Not this week. I've set that aside for a difficult day with Mum.'

He sobered immediately. 'I guess it has to be done. Can I be of any help?'

Gail shook her head. 'I'm afraid this is one thing I have to sort out for myself.'

'I'll book a table for the three of us to dine at Anton's in the hope that your day is successful.'

'It will be,' she told him with more conviction than she felt.

'I'll believe it when I see you both walk arm in arm through the door into Anton's.'

*   *   *

In the end, persuading her mother to accept the truth was somewhat easier than either Gail or Matt had anticipated.

Initially she refused point-blank to look at the transcript of the inquest or listen to anything Gail had to say.

So, acting on Matt's suggestion, she told her about their engagement.

After listening for some time to her mother ranting the usual accusations against him, she told her quietly, 'None of that is true, Mum. I know it now, and if you would only read this, you would too.'

'He might be able to convince you, but he'll never, never convince me.' When her mother snatched the papers from her, intending to shred them, Gail captured her hand firmly between her own and said quietly, 'I love you very much, Mum, but if it's a choice between staying with you or going with Matt, I'm afraid I'd have no choice but to go.'

Her mother's anger turned to self-pity then and as she wept piteously she repeatedly demanded, 'How could you, Gail? How could you, my only remaining child, behave in this way?'

Gail waited for her sobs to quieten before telling her. 'Because I love Matt and I want to be with him. And I think George would be happy to know that I love the best friend he ever had. George would be the first to admit it was his mistake. That was something I still remember and admire him for—he never tried to shift the blame. Now are you going to read these, or shall I take them with me?'

It took time several more hours of cajoling before Mrs Peters agreed to read them properly and eventually shame-facedly admit that she hadn't allowed herself to accept that George could do anything that might warrant criticism. So she had believed what she'd wanted to believe.

Incredibly she then disclosed that she had suspected Gail had a soft spot for Matt all those years ago and the moment she'd heard they'd met up again she'd feared this might happen.

'So you weren't surprised when I told you we were engaged?'

'Not really.'

Noticing the tears flowing down her mother's cheeks, Gail gathered her into her arms and hugged her.

'I'm so happy for you, Gail.' She looked up through her tears. 'I never thought I'd hear myself say that, but I really mean it even if I wouldn't admit it until now.'

Gail was crying too. It had taken the whole of Saturday for her to reach that point and she was emotionally exhausted, but for Matt's sake she had been determined to persevere.

Hearing the dining room clock strike seven, she freed her mother and checked her watch. 'Matt has booked a table at Anton's for eight. We're going to get all glammed up and celebrate our engagement. OK?'

'He won't want me there.'

'He's doing it so that we can all be together and put the past behind us.'

Her mother was still apprehensive but Gail told her quietly, 'There'll be no recriminations. Matt says you're the only mother he has ever known.'

They all shed a few tears that evening and the conversation was stilted until Gail announced that she and Matt intended to marry the first weekend in September and that she would have an eight-year-old bridesmaid.

'I can make all the dresses. And the cake,' Mrs Peters told them, her eyes shining. 'But who is this girl? Not— not your—your daughter, is it?'

Gail shook her head with a smile. 'Emma is an orphan like Matt was and we're hoping to give her a home. You could meet her tomorrow if you're not doing anything else.'

'You know I never am—'

'We'll soon change that, Mrs Peters,' Matt told her with a warmth that tugged at Gail's heartstrings. She grasped his hand tightly in hers.

It must have struck a chord with her mother as well, for she said to Matt, 'Do please call me Peggy.'

She grasped her mother's hand on the other side. 'Thanks, Mum.'

When she heard about their plans for Emma, and then met her, as Matt had predicted Peggy Peters' life took on a whole new meaning.

Her friendship with the little girl ignored the generation gap, even seemed to benefit from it. Within a short space of time, she offered to make a home for Emma until Matt and Gail had had a chance to settle as newly-weds.

Diane was happy for them to give it a try and it worked better than any of them would have believed.

When the time came for Gail to leave the chest clinic, all the staff were sorry to see her go, but they knew they would be meeting her again.

'You work hard for those membership exams,' Pam told her, 'and come back as Matt's registrar as soon as possible.'

'Maybe. If it's right for my career.'

Later, as Matt helped her to move into her new room at St John's, he told her, 'It's unbelievable what has happened to us both in just six months.'

'I'm still trying to catch my breath.'

'I still find it incredible what your mother and Emma are doing for one another. It doesn't look as if there's going to be a need for professional help for either of them, does it?'

Gail shook her head. 'We are *so* lucky, Matt—it means I can start my new post without worrying about after-school arrangements for Emma. *And* I should find the time to study.'

'Between other things,' he whispered suggestively. 'You did make sure Medical Personnel knew you were having time off for the wedding, didn't you?'

'Stop worrying, Matt. With Graham as your best man there's no problem there. I know I don't want you to pull strings for me in the future but I'm glad you did this for me.' She grinned slyly. 'You know, I'm going to quite enjoy working with him 'cos if anything he's even better looking and more accommodating than you are.'

'It sounds a good job he's already married to Venetia,' he muttered darkly.

She murmured silkily, 'You're surely not jealous, are you?'

'You look like a princess,' Emma breathed shyly as Gail came slowly down the stairs of her mother's Cricklewood house, her cream silk dress flaring out into a train that followed her every step.

'If I'm a princess, Emma, you're a little queen in that green dress.'

Mrs Peters came fussily down the stairs behind her. 'Look. Aren't the flowers magnificent?' She handed Emma a small posy and Gail a bouquet that smelled like a summer's day and had trailing greenery that matched the trim on her dress.

'Don't sit down, Gail. You'll have creases at the back. The photographer'll be here in a minute. And the car.'

'I'll have to sit down on the way to the church, Mum.'

'Of course you will, dear, but you'll have had some photographs taken by then.'

Gail smiled impishly at Emma, but said nothing and moved out to greet the photographer. While he set up his cameras she lifted her face to the September sun that was so unexpected after the torrential rain of the days before.

When the photographs were taken, she waved to the neighbours she had known since childhood, and her mother helped her into the back seat of the vintage green limousine which was waiting patiently at the gate.

Emma climbed in beside her while Mrs Peters locked up the house and took the front seat beside the driver.

*   *   *

As they processed down the aisle, Matt turned to look at the three women who from that day forward would be his family.

When Gail arrived at his side, he welcomed her with a broad, loving smile and murmured, 'You look absolutely stunning.' He was rewarded by a pair of loving blue eyes smiling up at him.

When the minister asked who was giving the bride for marriage, Matt turned and met Peggy Peters' happy gaze as she clearly and proudly announced, 'I do,' and before she turned to take her seat at the front of the congregation he gave her an encouraging wink.

Emma played her part in the service with equal aplomb, taking Gail's bouquet at the right time and lifting the train of her dress as they moved forward to kneel and then to sign the register.

He felt so proud of his new family and as he took the rings from Graham, who was an exemplary best man, he knew George was also there, as best man in spirit.

The invited congregation in the small chapel was swelled by every member of Lizzie's staff who could scrape even an hour off duty and they almost lifted the roof with their cheer when the minister pronounced them married and told Matt he could kiss his wife.

Later, as they relaxed in their enormous twelfth-century hotel bedroom, Gail said ruefully to Matt, 'There was no fear of Mum being upset at losing a daughter today, was there? They are so close now I can see Emma refusing to ever move in with us.'

Matt lifted the bottle of champagne that nestled in a bucket of ice beside him. After thoughtfully pouring them both another glass, he said, 'You wouldn't mind, would you? It would mean you'd be free to continue your career. For a little while, at least.'

'I'd like that—' she kissed him '—but only if I can choose my consultant.'

He laughed. 'I thought you'd done that already.'

MILLS & BOON®

Makes any time special™

Mills & Boon publish 29 new titles every month. Select from...

Modern Romance™   Tender Romance™

Sensual Romance™

Medical Romance™   Historical Romance™

MAT2

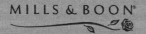

MILLS & BOON®

Medical Romance™

THE ELUSIVE DOCTOR *by Abigail Gordon*

Ambitious Dr Nina Lombard did not want to be in the quaint village of Stepping Dearsley! But now that she was working for Dr Robert Carslake, Nina found that she had a reason to stay...

A SURGEON'S REPUTATION *by Lucy Clark*

Dr James Crosby has made his attraction clear to Dr Holly Mayberry but something from his past is holding him back. When James's reputation is put on the line Holly knows she has a chance to win his trust and his heart...

DELIVERING LOVE *by Fiona McArthur*

New Author

Poppy McCrae has always used complementary therapies in her work as a midwife. Paediatrician Jake Sheppard thoroughly disapproves of her methods. Can Poppy persuade Jake to accept her and her beliefs?

On sale 2nd February 2001

0101/03b